SUFFLED
OFF

A GHOST'S MEMOIR
BOOK 1

SUFFLED OFF

A GHOST'S MEMOIR
BOOK 1

ROBERT J. MCCARTER

Little Hummingbird Publishing
Flagstaff, AZ

Shuffled Off: A Ghost's Memoir, Book 1

Cover images ©iStockPhoto.com, KarenMassier and © Lymedia | Dreamstime

Version 1.2, August 2017 (new cover)
Version 1.1, October 2013
Version 1.0, October 2011

ISBN: 978-0-9642096-2-6

Find out more about this book at: www.ShuffledOff.com
Visit Robert's website at: www.RobertJMcCarter.com

Published by:
Little Hummingbird Publishing
P.O. Box 23518
Flagstaff, AZ 86002
www.LittleHummingbird.com

Little Hummingbird Publishing is a division of Arapas, Inc. Find more about Arapas at: www.Arapas.com.

Dedicated to

Wayne, Jeff, Bob, Paul, Steve, Trish, Katherine, Lew, Emerson, Tyra, Bear, Moet and all the other two-footed and four-footed friends that have shuffled off before me. I'll be seeing you all someday, and it best be a party!

"For in that sleep of death what dreams may come, when
we have shuffled off this mortal coil"
Hamlet: Act III, Scene I, by William Shakespeare

Prologue

Tamara Watson was nervous. "What if they don't believe us?" she asked Jin Shi.

"If they don't believe us, we've been duped; I mean they are both all over that thing," Jin answered, indicating the large stack of paper Tamara held in her lap.

She thought it a bit silly, but Jin had insisted. They carried the words on paper, because Jin would not risk losing control of it by transferring it electronically. The source copy was on an isolated network, the backups heavily encrypted, the reading copies on paper.

Jin was driving them down Interstate 10, the road laid out in front of them like a pair of black ribbons running through the scrub desert. They were leaving the outskirts of Tucson heading northwest towards Phoenix.

"I know, I know. It's just..." Tamara said, clutching the paper in her lap.

"What? You know we have to do this, otherwise no one will believe a word in that." Jin gripped the steering wheel, his knuckles turning white.

"This is it," Tamara said pointing across the median at

the two lanes going the other way.

"Huh?"

"Right here is where it happened. Where they..." She trailed off not finishing her thought.

"Look, we did our homework; we have validated as many facts in there as we can. That wreck, Ms. Smithson's fall, the incident over by Picacho Peak. We have to take the next step and interview the witnesses."

"I know," Tamara said quietly, staring straight ahead.

"Besides, he told us to do this. There's no way I'm going against him."

"Jin!"

"You read that! You know what he can do."

"Jin! JJ is not like that. He wasn't trying to hurt anyone."

"Yeah, well he did," Jin said, looking around as he added, "he could be here, right now." They were alone in the car.

Tamara sighed refusing to engage again in Jin's paranoia. If she were being truthful, she would have to admit to some of it herself—there was no place to hide from him. They drove on for a few minutes in silence.

"Isn't this what you wanted all along?" Jin finally asked.

"Well... Yes. I just didn't expect the first transmissions to come from someone we knew. I... I wasn't expecting to lose a friend."

"Before you came along," Jin said, "my project was straight forward; you are the one that wanted to add all these metaphysical components."

"It's not like you objected—all those dollars dancing in your eyes."

"Tam, what's wrong with that? We'll probably make millions off the book alone, not to mention movie rights."

"It was never about that," Tamara insisted.

"For you, that is."

"Damn it Jin, you know why I did this." She was tired of this conversation; they had had it before, and would undoubtedly have it again. She didn't want to talk about her fiancé and what happened after he died. She didn't want to go poking around in the grief that still felt surprisingly raw two years later.

"I know Tam," Jin said. "Look, I'm sorry. I really liked JJ too. I am sorry he's gone. I'm sorry it took him dying for us to get that." Again he glanced at the stack of paper in her lap.

"It's OK Jin, we're just both nervous." Consulting the GPS she added, "This is our exit coming up."

They got off the highway and drove along the frontage road past some rusted water tanks until they came to a dirt road.

"Here," Tamara said, "turn here. There is the rusted wagon wheel he mentioned."

Jin turned the car down the dirt road and they slowly drove out into the desert until they came to a lone trailer sitting on a slight rise. In front of it was a large red tow truck with "Sal's Towing" painted in white letters on the side. Next to it were two cars, one covered with a tarp, the other a badly damaged wreck. Behind the vehicles stood a small shed.

"Well, here we are, let's get this done," Jin said as he shut the car off and got out.

Nate Luca emerged from the trailer. He was a large man, about thirty years old, with a barrel chest, thick arms, and short cropped black hair. He was dressed in jeans and a white t-shirt. He reminded Tamara of a bear. He always seemed to be so sweet, but she imagined that if you crossed him that, like a bear, he would be fearsome.

"Jin. Tamara. Did you have any trouble finding me?" Nate asked.

"Nope," Jin said shaking the big man's hand. "Good to see you again Nate, thanks for agreeing to this."

"You're welcome, but I have no idea what I have agreed to."

"Sorry about the secrecy, but we have to follow certain protocols."

Nate shrugged as if lifting the weight of his questions up and letting them roll off his broad shoulders.

"Is Mrs. Lynch here?" Jin asked.

Nate said that she was and showed them in. When they entered, Janet Lynch, a short middle-aged woman with graying hair was in the tiny kitchen vigorously scrubbing down the counters. She looked up, startled when the door opened, in mid-swipe with a rag in her hand. She said with a smile, "Sorry, nervous habit. Hope you don't mind."

"Mi casa, su casa," Nate said with a grin.

She wiped her hands off and came around into the small living room embracing Tamara, her lips brushing her cheek. "You look good dear. I like the new haircut, it suits you."

Tamara smiled, her hands touching her shoulder length hair. "Thank you." She was impressed that Mrs. Lynch noticed; she had only met her a few times.

"And you Jin, thank you for coming," Janet said as she embraced him.

"Thank you Mrs. Lynch," Jin said, "we really appreciate you doing this."

"Janet, it's Janet."

"OK. Janet."

"Better. So what exactly are we doing?"

"Sorry, but I can't tell you yet," Jin said. "I know it is

strange, but first I need you to sign these non-disclosure agreements and affidavits, and I need to set up our video equipment."

Tamara talked them through the agreements while Jin busied himself setting up two cameras, one pointed at Nate and the other one at Janet. "OK Tam, you take it from here," Jin said, moving behind the cameras and starting the recordings.

Tamara stood, wiping her hands on her black skirt. "What I have here," she said holding the large stack of paper in her hands, "is what we believe are..." She paused, clearing her throat. "Excuse me, I'm really nervous."

"Don't be dear," Janet said, "just spit it out."

"Do either of you know what Jin and I are doing at the university?" Tamara asked.

"No," Janet said.

"JJ mentioned something about some fancy electronic shielding," Nate added.

"OK," Tamara said, "the shielding is part of it. We have created a way that..." She stopped speaking again, her hands gripping the paper harder. Taking a deep breath she continued looking at Janet. "Forget the technology part, what I have here is a document written by... written by your son."

"OK. So why all the secrecy?" Janet asked.

"Because of when he wrote it," Tamara said.

"When he wrote it?" Janet asked

"Yes," Tamara said licking her lips, "he wrote this starting last October."

Janet's face fell, her sagging skin adding years to her apparent age. Nate's eyes widened, his head slowly nodding up and down.

"But he died in—" Janet began.

"In August," Tamara continued. "Yes. That is why we are being so secretive about this."

"What?" Janet asked. She was swaying slightly as if dizzy. "What are you saying?"

Tamara took a moment to answer, speaking slowly, "I am saying that your son wrote this after he died."

"What are you trying to do to me? I will not listen to this!" Janet surged to her feet, her face flush, her eyes tearing up.

Nate reached up and took her hand and said, "I think we should listen to them."

"What?" Janet said, looking down at the big man.

"I have reason to believe them," Nate said softly.

"What!?" Janet asked, shaking her head.

"Please, just listen," Nate said, his voice still, soft, and even.

Janet sat down, but kept a hold of Nate's hand. "Excuse me dear," she said to Tamara, "please continue."

"I am going to read this to you. At certain points I will stop and ask you to comment on the accuracy of the events described, and to add any remarks you might have. Any questions?"

Both mutely shook their heads "no."

Tamara, still nervous, took a deep breath trying to clear her head and began reading.

Transmission #1
Received 2010/10/19 03:14:03

When someone dies, the world doesn't stop. It seems like it should, but it doesn't. Sure if it's a famous person, or a grisly murder, there is a period of piranha-like activity on the part of media. But that's not stopping, that is just business as usual in the land of the twenty-four hour news cycle. Even then it settles down quickly and everyone gets back to their shaky, unsure life.

It would be useful if it did stop. You know, take a moment, get your bearings, and deal with the practical and emotional details that engulf a death. But no, no stopping, no break, you just gotta continue your drunkard's walk down the path of life.

When I died, the world didn't stop, not a bit. I wasn't expecting it to, but it would've been nice, you know?

The death effect is kind of like throwing a stone into a pond: a famous person is like a rock—it stirs things up; an everyman, like me, is more like a tiny pebble—it effects the immediate surrounding but has no discernable effect on the whole. In the end neither one really changes things much;

the world doesn't stop. Life goes on.

My ma was a mess, it rocked her world—"a parent shouldn't outlive her child," and all that junk. My sister Jean spent about three days contemplating her own mortality and just went back to business as usual—the college social scene is all consuming. Nate, now he was ripped up. We've been joined at the hip since junior high, and my exit really sent him spinning.

I used to wish there was a sign that a person was going to leave soon. Like a light over their head that they can't see, and no one tells them about, but everyone around them sees and can act on. You know: be nice, spend time with them, tell them what you've got to tell them. My dad died quick, a heart attack, and it left me devastated, wishing I had said and done things different towards the end. You know the end is gonna come, but when it arrives it arrives so damn quick.

But now that it was me, I would want to have seen the light over my head too. I would have liked to look up Rhiannon and told her how sorry I was. I would have ditched work and taken a good long vacation. I would have slept a lot less, and lived a lot more.

So now you must be thinking who's the mouthy guy writing from beyond the pale. Woooooooooooo. At least that's what I would be thinking, I have no idea what you are thinking, I ain't no mind reader.

OK, so my name is Joseph Jeffery Lynch, JJ to my friends. I am twenty-nine years old, and I am dead. Well mostly dead. Actually I don't really know. The body is gone, but I seem to still have a sense of myself, of who I am, even without it. Is that alive, or is that dead? Is that un-dead? I guess if you had to choose a word for my condition, you would choose the word "ghost." Woooooooooooo.

Scared yet? I would be if I were you. What I have to tell has its scary parts, its happy parts, and its sad parts—just like life. Is life scary to you? To me it was, sometimes, and I can now say the same thing about death.

Wonder how a ghost can write? Good question. I am using some new technology here at the University of Arizona (UA) that allows me to "type." Part of the SECI program. Never heard of it? It stands for the Search for Extra-Corporeal Intelligence. What SETI is to aliens, SECI is to ghosts.

Don't be surprised if you haven't heard of it. It is kind of a ghost project (pun intended) running underneath a more respectable project studying lightweight electromagnetic (EM) shielding. Now I don't fully understand the technology, but here I am the first beta tester.

I graduated college (barely, and with a liberal arts degree at that), but because of circumstances, that I imagine we'll get into later, I never moved on from my college job. I worked as a janitor at UA and among other things, I cleaned up the small lab that Jin Shi and Tamara Watson run the SECI program out of. They would often be there late and we would talk about things: about ghosts, and death, and the nature of life. The basic theory is this: consciousness exists outside of the body, the body being an amplifier for that consciousness. Jin and Tam were trying to figure out another type of amplifier—so was born SECI.

"Look," Tam told me once, "every religion in the world believes consciousness goes on beyond the corporeal form, exists separate from the corporeal form. They can't all be wrong; we are just trying to find a way to communicate with that realm."

Tam, she was always good to me, and she was cute, so

I kinda had a crush on her. Big lips, lots up top, but not much of a butt (but I wouldn't kick her out of bed for that!). She also had this vulnerability, this deep need; it was clear she was doing SECI for very personal reasons.

"Imagine it, JJ," Jin said, he always had this glint in his eye when he talked about this part. "How much would this be worth? Talk to the dearly departed; solve murders; find out the secrets of the great beyond." Clearly the monetary ramifications were what got him going.

"So how does it work?" I asked.

"Our theory revolves around detecting non-random, patterned EM fluctuations in a highly EM shielded space," Tam explained. "Our SECI Chamber will theoretically shield all external EM radiation, so that any EM it picks up will have to be from within the chamber, from an extra-corporeal. The chamber will have in-depth instructions for the earth-bound extra-corporeal entity so they know what patterns to create to communicate with us."

"Huh?" It was all beyond me; I'm just a janitor with a liberal arts degree.

I lived about a mile south of UA, in a little studio apartment. It was old, not in a good part of town, but serviceable. Couldn't do much better on what I made.

I mostly used my skateboard to get around. Yeah, I know, a man of my age—what can I say? I was without four-wheeled motorized transport.

About two months ago—give or take, time is tough to measure right now—I was headed home on a blistering August night at about 2 a.m. I was kicking my way south when a black Audi A4 plowed into me.

The car, full of drunk undergrads, veered to avoid something (or nothing, they were seriously altered), hopped the curb, hit me and plowed us all into a Mickey D's. I was out quick, and my body expired some minutes later pinned to a kiddie jungle gym.

That undergrad's car was equipped with airbags leaving the passengers relatively unharmed. I, on the other hand, was smushed like a bug against a windshield.

The EMTs tried to revive me, they tried hard. They got me out and hauled me back to Saint Mother of the Weeping Virgin (or something like that), but it was no use.

It wasn't bad, dying that is. I've had headaches that hurt more. What was hard was watching it all. As soon as the car plowed into me, I popped out and kind of floated (I guess) along and watched the whole bloody procedure.

One plastered, Barbie-blond co-ed stumbled out of the car, looked at what was left of me and said, "Oh my God, that is so gross!"

The driver, a GQ pretty-boy, called someone, Daddy I presume, and said, "It wasn't my fault, you've got to get me out of this." His voice shook and his face was pale.

There were people screaming, others with broken bones and injuries, weeping women, and one patron barfing up their recently consumed meat-like-substance.

As the firemen pulled back the car, it was surreal watching my body slide to the floor like a wet rag, my eyes open and vacant, my limbs bent at odd angles. So quick, so sudden, one moment alive, the next dead and all that is left is the meat body I used to inhabit. Like a candle being snuffed out, like a marionette getting its strings cut, like the air rushing out of a balloon, like a... Too many metaphors? Maybe, but man was it sudden, and that suddenness was bizarre and hard to accept.

The paramedics went right to it, following their

procedures: mobilizing my neck; shocking my heart; pumping me full of meds; hauling me off in the ambulance. I was attached to my body by some sort of silver cord. When the body was moved, I just got dragged along.

The ambulance was cool; I had never been in one. All that gear, and it was fast. We tore through the streets, sirens blaring, weaving around what little traffic there was. Kind of made me wish I had been an ambulance jockey instead of a janitor. What a ride!

Interview Transcript
Janet Lynch / Nate Luca: Part 1

Subjects: Janet Lynch (mother of the deceased) and Nate Luca (friend of the deceased)

Interviewed By: Tamara Watson

Date: 2/08/2011 11 a.m.

Janet: (crying) Ohhhh.

Nate: Ma, are you OK, do you need a minute?

Janet: No, no, let's keep going. Let's just get this over with.

Nate: (to Tamara after a period of silence) Did you want us to comment now?

Tamara: If you have something to say, yes. We received the story in a series of transmissions, and in between those transmissions is a convenient place to comment.

Nate: And what kind of feedback are you looking for?

Tamara: Mostly the accuracy of events described, particularly the paranormal events. That and whether this sounds like him, like JJ.

Janet: (nods her head up and down).

Nate: Yeah, it sounds like him—he would have loved the

ambulance ride. But how did he write this?

Tamara: It's technical and complicated, just think of it as a kind of typewriter. He actually describes the process in detail later.

Nate: Typewriter? (looking surprised) He and I...

Tamara: Excuse me?

Nate: Never mind (shaking head).

Janet: What is it Nate?

Nate: We... I.... (sigh) Let's just wait. I bet JJ writes about it, it will be easier that way.

Transmission #2
Received 2010/10/20 02:15:26

Sorry about that, got tired I guess. This is hard work: forming the shapes clearly enough to be translated into letters.

Jin, you called it. The feedback system works well. If I couldn't see the result of my efforts this just wouldn't work. Sorry if the prose is a bit rough, it's just too much to go back and edit it into something prettier.

I can't think that it matters to you though. I bet there was jumping for joy when you saw the first intelligible bit come in. Did that bottle of champagne finally get opened? Sorry I wasn't here to witness it.

So where was I? Oh yeah, death by car at the Mickey D's.

When my dad passed, I got my head shrunk for a while and the shrink, she told me about the five stages of grief. As I recall they are: Denial, Anger, Deals, Depression, and Acceptance. I think that is it, normally I would just look it up, but that's not going to work right now.

JJ's Things That Suck About Being Dead (JJTTSABD) #1: *Can't use the net to look stuff up and pretend you are smarter than you really are.*

So I think there are stages, similar stages, to dying; at least for me.

Stage 1: Shock, aka Denial, aka wtf just happened?

So watching myself die, the self-absorbed bleating of my killers, the wild ride to Saint Mother of All That is Virginal, watching the heroic efforts to save me—was Stage #1: Shock, and shock is just one variant of the larger (much larger) area of Denial.

There was this weird detachment. It was me, but it wasn't me. As I watched those doctors and nurses trying to pummel my body back to life, I kept trying to talk to them. I said, "Hey, I'm right here, it's OK. I'm not really dead." Shattered hip; broken ribs; lacerated bowels; punctured spleen; blood loss; head trauma; and on and on it went. One at a time they accessed and tried to stabilize my injuries. They got the heart going a few times, but never for very long.

After a while I started getting worried—what if they succeeded? I didn't want back in that thing, man that would just be hell. So I kept telling them that it was OK, that they should let me go. Eventually they did. The process, though, was gratifying. It was amazing seeing my life cared for to such a degree by a room full of strangers.

At this stage I was attached to my body—I went where it did, just got dragged along. After the heroics were over I was left there for some time, just me and my body. Just me and me.

I don't remember much of that time, but I developed a little mantra that pulled me through: wtf, wtf, wtf, wtf, wtf... For how long I have no idea. How could this have happened? That might have been crossing tentatively over to Stage 2: Anger. But believe me, it was way more shock than anger.

When anger came there was no denying it.

The morgue was next, a cold sterile room where my body was shoved into a drawer. There were three others there with me. I guess you would call them ghosts, but I was still having a hard time with that. All three were wispy floating forms with silver cords leading to a drawer. Two were completely out of it, looking gape jawed and stupid, just wandering around. The third's name was Jesus.

"Hey fresh meat, what happened to you?" he asked.

I would have jumped out of my skin, if I had skin. I don't know why, but I just wasn't expecting that.

"Huh?" I mumbled.

"Oh man, not another bardo-brain," he said.

"What?"

"What a waste of space. Can't you bring me someone to talk to?" He looked up as he said this.

"Are you talking to me?"

"Praise be to Guadalupe! Yeah man, I'm talking to you." With a big smile on his face he added, "My name is Hey-zeus."

"Hey-zeus, you mean as in Gee-zus?"

"Difference in pronunciation. If you would be so kind, please call me Hey-zeus. Although I am a mighty handsome guy, I don't want to be confused with the big fellow." He pointed up.

I am not sure if he was handsome or not: his dancing eyes were brown; his face was plain and kind looking; and he had a big full mustache wiggling above his smile.

"Oh yeah, sure. My name is JJ." I would have extended my hand, but it wasn't quite like that. I had a sense of form, but it wasn't steady, especially regarding limbs. Jesus's face was clear, but the rest of his body came in and out of...

hmmm... focus I guess, depending on what he was doing. I suppose it was the same for mine.

Turns out Jesus had been there a while. He was an illegal and as such his body had not been claimed yet. Jesus was a bounty hunter that had snuck across the border chasing a murderer. He wasn't like a normal bounty hunter, at least not what I thought normal bounty hunters did; he also tried to "show them the light of the divine Mother Mary" before he turned them in.

Next came, what I have come to know is, a standard ritual among the dead.

"So, how'd you die?" Jesus asked.

"Pinned to the jungle gym at a Mickey D's by a car full of ripped college kids."

"Nice! Wow." He seemed to be impressed.

"How did you die?" I asked. It only seemed polite to reciprocate.

"Ice pick to my left eye," he answered pointing to it. "I had the perp caught and cuffed, not sure how he came up with the pick."

There was a period of awkward silence for a while after that. I mean, what do you say? So sorry we're both dead; what the hell do we do now? I guess I must have started to glaze over.

"Don't go bardo on me man!" Jesus yelled. "Just keep moving man, and keep talking. That will help you settle in to... well you know." With that he walked to the other end of the room and right through the doors.

I tried to follow him, but after I got about two feet further I was snapped back all the way into my drawer. I got out of there quick; I didn't want to be in there with my body.

JJTTSABD #2: *Being attached to a dead chunk of rotting meat really sucks.*

When I got out, Jesus was back and he just chuckled. "You've got to keep practicing. I met a fellow a few days ago that could move independently of his body; he didn't have the silver cord."

"Really?"

"Yup, you might see him too. He likes to come down here and mess with the bardo-brains, they're easy to scare."

"Bardo-brains?"

"Yeah, those poor suckers," he pointed at the two others wandering around gape jawed and unaware, "are stuck in their own private hell—can't get out and move on. Banquo, that's his name, says he is doing them a service, trying to shock them back to this world. Me, I don't know, just kinda looks like he is scaring the shit out of them."

"Banquo? That's a weird name," I said.

Jesus shrugged, "Well he's a *strange* fellow."

We talked a lot about everything, and when that got old we would turn to trading insults. I would give him shit about his name, and he would say: "At least I didn't die at Mickey D's kiddy land." I would come back with: "And what kind of bounty hunter were you? Getting ice-picked by some coked-up, handcuffed perp." He would then call me a red-neck, and I would call him a wetback. It was good natured and it was fun. Until it wasn't, that is. Eventually someone would hit pay-dirt sending one of us close to going bardo and the other would have to pull them out while staying in safe conversational territory.

Transmission #3
Received 2010/10/21 04:23:15

So Jesus really saved me there. Kept me from going bardo, which I guess I would have done if he hadn't been there. I was with him for maybe a day before I got transferred to the mortuary.

They pulled the body—yeah, I wasn't calling it mine anymore but "the," trying to view it more as an anchor—out of the drawer onto a gurney and into a meat-wagon. I guess you could look on this as the first whisper of Stage #5: Acceptance. I was starting to accept the fact that hunk-o-meat was not "me."

As I was being dragged along with the body I shouted to Jesus, "Thanks Jesus, you really saved me!" Pronouncing his name as Gee-zus.

That made him grin as he floated along besides me, "Just keep talking, keep moving. Stay out of bardo-land and you'll be OK."

"You too bro. Thanks, I owe you."

Jesus hit his limit and couldn't go any further. As we parted I shouted, "Jesus saves!"

The mortuary sucked. I was stuck, attached to that which used to be me, watching this weird guy with thick old fashioned glasses work on my body.

He first checked for a pulse (yeah bub, I am seriously dead), stripped and washed the body, flexed and massaged the arms and legs until they would lie flat, sewed up the injuries, and injected fluids into it. Then came trying to make it look like it wasn't dead. Only problem was, he was making my meat-face look scary as shit. Some sort of android version of what I once was.

I can't believe my mom was going to do the open casket thing. I guess it is good for some folks: seeing the dead chunk of meat helps them let go. Me, I never wanted that. Just burn me quick and dump the ashes somewhere. Nothing left, no place for folks to go and cry.

I slipped briefly into Stage #4: Depression, but thanks to Jesus I was good at catching the signs. See, depression leads to bardo-brain, and I was more scared of that than I was of being dead. Without Jesus here to save me I had to keep myself on track.

So when I felt that depression coming on, I just started singing as loud as I could, the song *Don't Fear the Reaper*.

The worse it got, the louder I sang, and I marched slowly away from "the meat that used to be me" stretching out the cord. When I got there I could only move four feet away. After a few hours of singing and marching (and making up really lyrics staring your's truly). I stretched it to eight feet.

I was trying to break the record, went too far, and got snapped right back to my body. My head, such as it was,

was taking up the same space as the spectacled embalmer dude. He was applying rouge (yeah, rouge!) to my cheeks. It freaked me out and I felt the bardo approaching fast, so I started singing louder than ever.

Embalmer dude—let's call him Ed for short—jerked up and looked around, scratching his head. Did he hear me? Not sure, so I got right next to his ear and shouted as loud as I could, "Don't fear the reaper, JJ is the man!"

Sure enough, Ed jumped, just a bit, and looked around. "What was that?" he whispered.

I was ecstatic, and started running around with my hands in the air as if I had just won an Olympic gold medal. I wasn't really watching where I was going and popped out into the next room where another piece of meat was laid out in a coffin with folks lining up to pay their respects.

Not only had I communicated with someone, I had extended my leash! As I found out later, feeling good made things work better on this side too.

The situation in the room was tense: folks in small intimate knots talking quietly; a small line of people parading past the body muttering their goodbyes, most crying or with tears in their eyes; and one older lady, the wife I presume, wailing in a corner, awkwardly comforted by what I assume were her children.

That is another tough thing about grieving. The one with the greatest loss is the one that receives the comfort, kind of like a pecking order. The wife lost the most, so the children comforted her, when they were ripped up inside too.

There were also a few mortuary suits standing there: impeccably groomed, good posture, and appropriately dour expressions on their faces. How do you do a job like that? To be surrounded constantly by other people's grief and yet retain a shred of your own joy, or sanity at the very least.

Yup, I woke up happy today, smiling with a spring in my step. Then I went to work and had to transform myself into a conciliatory zombie. Yuck.

And then, finally, was the ghost. Hovering around the coffin was a bardo-ed, gape mouthed extra-corporeal. From what I heard folks saying he had a massive stroke and went fast.

I walked up (OK, hovered) to him and said, "Hey pops, how'd you die?" His expression didn't change, those eyes hollow and far off. Then I had an idea: since he was still closely attached to his body, maybe...

"Look at this old fart. I bet he has a mouth full of crowns in there, probably some of them gold. I love gold!" I glanced over but nothing had changed. "I'm just gonna reach in here and see what I can find." I gingerly stuck my hand into his mouth and made a good show of it.

That did it, his eyes popped into focus, and he said "Hey!" He swooped towards me, passing through those that were standing there looking at the meat that was him. One of them shivered, and I felt what I can only describe as a cold breeze rushing past.

I pulled my hand out and said, "No harm pops, no harm. My name is JJ. So how did you die?"

He stopped, looked around and moaned, "Dead, I'm dead? How can I be dead? I'm not dead!" A look of horror came over his face and, pop, back to bardo-land for him.

I left; he just didn't seem to be ready for what had happened to him, thoroughly engrossed in the denial/shock stage. I spent the rest of the day just outside the building. I tried to go further, but couldn't. So I loitered near the entrance yelling in people's ears seeing how many I could reach.

Not many, but a few seemed to sense something. Not what I was saying or anything, but they sensed something. One old biddy shivered, a man with a hearing aid twiddled with it like it had squealed or something.

Not much of a way to pass time, but at least I wasn't stuck in there with my meat.

When I went outside, I discovered this was not just a mortuary, but a cemetery too. That freaked me out a bit, probably lots of ghosts around here. And you know, just because you are a ghost doesn't mean you want to run into a bunch of other ghosts. The bardo-brained newly dead were bad enough, but what must it be like for a spirit stuck in a place like this for a decade or a century?

This place was on the corner of Miracle and Oracle. You think the roads were named that way when they built the place? Seems like two strange names. With tall trees and green grass it was surprisingly lush for Tucson. At least it was a lovely place, and peaceful at the moment.

I hung around outside, and poked around inside, carefully avoiding my meat, but not much exciting happened. I did learn a few things.

First of all those mortuary suits got pretty weird when they were on break and no one (but us ghosts) were around.

The tall one, Hal I think, did a dead-on impression of the grieving widow for his coworkers, complete with crying, carrying on and a grief soaked east coast accent.

Alice, the only chick on duty, was a foulmouthed, chain smoking witch when she was out of sight of the patrons. She kept going on about how much she would drink at night, and how sick she would get. Later in my stay I caught her and Hal getting it on in the embalming room—sick.

Ed, my embalmer, started to regale them with the gruesome details of just how messed up I was. I got out of there fast, planning to stay outside until everyone had gone home and the place was locked up.

I didn't take it personally. I've just got to imagine with a job like that you've got to blow the steam off any way you can.

Interview Transcript
Janet Lynch / Nate Luca: Part 2

Janet: (crying) Bardo? Meat? Jesus? What is all this? I don't understand.

Nate: Is this really necessary? All these details? Can't we skip to the parts that you need us to comment on?

Tamara: I'm so sorry. This was JJ's request that we share this with you.

Nate: JJ? Request?

Tamara: Yes, he was very specific.

Nate: But why?

Tamara: He wanted you both to know that he was OK. His last transmission contained this request.

Nate: This is him being OK?

Tamara: (sighs) I know it is strange, this story, this journey. If you can, I think we should keep going. I think it will help.

Janet: OK (nodding).

Transmission #4
Received 2010/10/22 02:56:21

I had to take a break, but I think I am getting better at this; it is going faster at least.

One weird thing that happens; when I get really exhausted, I just go away. I have no idea what happens to me or where I am but some time later I come back and feel all groggy. Kind of like a deep dreamless sleep. It is referred to as "fading," I have seen other spirits do it, and that is what it looks like—they just slowly fade away.

I often wake up somewhere different from when I went to sleep, often not in good places. The other day I woke up in the middle of I-10 with a wall of traffic descending on me. I would have died, if I had not already been dead.

JJTTSABD #3: *Waking up at some random location and getting the shock of your life... err death, ... sucks.*

I don't like "fading," I just don't trust it. I guess I am afraid that I won't come back, that it will be the end. I think I went through a phase like that when I was a kid. I would fight sleeping as long as I could—I didn't trust it, I didn't want to miss anything, and I was afraid of not coming back.

That evening things got really interesting at the mortuary; I had a series of visitors.

First up was Marilyn. She arrived just as the sun was going down, the sunlight filtered through the dust and pollution bathed everything in a warm glow. She was well formed, wearing last century's fashionable clothing over her bulbous body. She was so well formed that for a bit I thought she was meat. That is until she walked right up to me and said, "Have you seen my cat?"

"You can see me?"

"Of course I can sonny," she said. "Have you seen my cat, Motor? He got himself lost again; he must be around here somewhere."

"So, how did you die?" I asked. Standard greeting, right? Just like in prison—hey bub, whatcha in for? Her face got pinched, her form started to break up, and her eyes got vacant. I scrambled, "Cat. Yeah, I saw a cat, just a little while ago." That snapped her back a bit, her hands reforming out of the vapor.

"You saw my cat?"

"Not sure if it was yours, but I did see a cat," I lied. "Hey lady, what's your name?" I backed up a bit, forcing her to follow me. Following Jesus's lead and getting her talking and moving.

"Marilyn. My name is Marilyn. I really need to find my cat." She paused and thought for a moment. She was fully back now. "Was it a black cat with lovely green eyes that you saw?"

"Yeah, I think so. I saw it run into the trees over there."

She waddled off and I didn't see her again until the same time the next day when we went through a similar routine. She didn't appear to recognize me; it seems like she was running the same track on repeat.

Shortly after Marilyn left, right after the sun went down, the noise started: stirring, rattling, whispers, mumbles, and more shocking noises. This place was surrounded: graves on two sides, and crypts on the other two.

At first I was curious, but when the moans turned into screams I started to get scared. I was really wishing Jesus was with me, and just when it was getting bad, I thought I heard him say, "Just keep talking, just keep walking."

I had no one to talk to, so I started back up with my butchered rendition of *Don't Fear the Reaper* and started running. At first I ran around the building, but the crypt sections just creeped me out too much so I kept to the front, running back and forth singing as loud as I could.

The red of the sunset deepened, and then before I knew it the light was gone. The night was moonless and the darkness dropped fast and heavy. As things darkened I saw shapes moving out in the cemetery. Perhaps my singing attracted them or perhaps they marched onto the mortuary every night, but either way they were coming closer and closer.

So I ran faster and sung louder—what else was I to do? I had no idea what they wanted, or how to defend myself. In retrospect I thought of them as "them." Not the same as me, but somehow separate and scary. Ghosts are scary, right? I didn't know what they could do to me, and that unknown was keeping me tottering on the brink.

I think he must have been yelling at me for a while before I noticed him.

"Boy! Boy! Screw your courage to the sticking-place."

He was the most well-formed spirit I had seen, although not an impressive form. He was short, bald, with a heavy belly.

I slowed down, and he repeated the phrase again: "Screw your courage to the sticking-place." The phrasing was odd, but his delivery resounding. I got the drift, and stopped long enough to look around.

The spirits were indeed moving into the mortuary, but they had given me, and this fellow, a wide berth. After I stopped, they moved in and took over the path I had been running, and I had no choice but to move closer to the man.

"So," I said, trying to insert some swagger into my voice, "how'd ya die?"

"Better, boy, better. My name is Banquo and I died in a plane crash." His void was deep, resonant, and calming.

"My name is JJ; I died pinned to a jungle gym at a Mickey D's."

"I thought I would find you here. Jesus told me that you might need some help."

"Jesus saves!" I couldn't resist pulling that one out again.

Banquo chuckled, "Indeed he does."

"Those... Those..." I stuttered, pointing towards the mortuary where the gang of spirits had gone.

"Just curious, for the most part. It is a small community, visitors are always an excitement. Come, we must talk."

Banquo guided me, much to my dismay, to the embalming room where my body, now dressed and fully "restored," was laid out. There were a few of the cemetery spirits examining my body, sticking their faces into my abdomen, fingers into my head.

"Hey!" I shouted. Just like the old fart that I messed

with, I felt proprietary about that piece of meat. It was *my* piece of meat.

"JJ, until you accept what happened, accept that you are dead, and that *thing* is no longer *you*, you will be chained to it."

Transmission #5
Received 2010/10/23 04:51:22

One of my first clear memories is of a wrench. My dad was a mechanic at a little place off of Ash in Globe, Arizona. My mom worked, and I guess they couldn't afford child care, so as soon as I was old enough my dad picked me up from school and took me to the garage until Ma got off of work.

That wrench was shiny silver and spotless. My dad's legs were sticking out from under the car he was working on, his beat up steel toe boots going back and forth like windshield wipers in synch with the music playing on the radio. I was handing him tools, and taking the ones he was done with—kinda like a surgical nurse.

His hand would pop out, all dirty, grease under his finger nails, and he'd say something like, "JJ give me the half-inch wrench." I would hand it to him, take it back when he was done, wipe it down, and put it back in its place.

It was like heaven. I was maybe six, but he only had to tell me once or twice what a tool was, and I would remember. It felt so good to be there knowing I was helping him. He was very particular about where the tools went and that they were kept clean. That clean part took a little longer for me to get, but soon I couldn't finish with a tool and not clean it up and put it back where it belonged.

I remember that wrench and that tool box, and the smell of grease and oil. The wrench was so bright and cool in my hand, the red tool box so big with all the little drawers. My dad was a really good mechanic, and I must have inherited some of that from him. I've always been good with my hands—tools just feel natural in them. Dad was a tough and demanding teacher; he really expected a lot of me, even when I was so young. I always appreciated that about him (when I wasn't busy hating it).

Professor Banquo was a tough teacher too, but I was not as graceful a student. I think the shock of it all did not lend me to being patient.

Banquo's lessons were: 1) Cutting the Cord; 2) Appearance Matters; 3) Awareness, Awareness, Awareness; 4) Traveling; and 5) This is Not the End.

Being a former professor of English Literature, his lessons were thorough, well planned, and difficult. That night and the next two he lectured me on "Cutting the Cord." He wouldn't go further, stating that if I couldn't do that, the rest didn't matter.

He also introduced me around and I found that most of the spirits in the cemetery were really no threat at all. Their form and personality varied wildly: from barely formed vapors that moaned and cried, to fully formed gentleman from the late 1800s that wanted nothing more than to debate the wisdom of Tesla's AC current versus Edison's DC. Some were crazy, others logical to a fault. Some stayed because they had to—they were buried here and still corded—some stayed because they wanted to.

Marilyn was an un-corded local obsessed with her missing cat. Most of the time there was really only one conversation you could have with her. Fredrick was the original owner and first mortician of the cemetery, who died in 1929—he liked to lord over the place, making introductions.

Jim was one of the original settlers in Tucson, he has been transferred over here from the overcrowded Presidio Cemetery. His constant companion was Jane, she used to run a speakeasy during prohibition. Those two made me wonder—if they were meat and looked at each other like that, I would think they were doing it every chance they got. Love in the afterlife? Kind of looked like it to me.

Banquo's lessons were full of information, but often not very practical. "You go on and on about this, but I am still not clear on how to cut the cord," I said to Banquo.

He paused, stroking his chin and said, "You have to want it, really want it: 'Decide that you want it more than you are afraid of it.'"

"Was that last part a Shakespeare quote?" I asked. He was awfully fond of quoting him; that "screw your courage to the sticking-place" bit he said when I met him is from Macbeth.

"No my dear boy, that didn't sound like the bard at all; that was Bill Cosby."

Was I afraid of parting with my body? I tried everything Banquo suggested: visualizations, affirmations, chants, rituals, but nothing worked. My cord got longer, but I couldn't break free.

The next evening after lessons, Banquo escorted me out to join the "Midnight Circle." The Circle, which formed at midnight, was kinda like what you meat folks do around a campfire. We all knew when it was midnight—we felt it in our... in our... well, in our bones.

Banquo was the king of the Circle—he was an amazing story teller and had many of Shakespeare's plays and other works memorized.

Everyone else had heard them all, many times, and often acted parts that went along with his tales, or chimed in for key lines—kinda like those nuts that still act out The Rocky Horror Picture Show. The first night I was there he did Hamlet. The "To be, or not to be" soliloquy was a great success; it just hit home. All of us hanging out on the other side, in the middle of a graveyard filled with ghosts, were heartily amused by Hamlet's contemplation of suicide and his fears of "what dreams may come when we have shuffled off this mortal coil."

The deaths were acted out with great gusto; the play being a tragedy, there were plenty. I mean everyone dies: Laertes stabs Hamlet with a poisoned blade; Hamlet fatally wounds Laertes; Gertrude drinks poison wine and croaks; and with his last breath Hamlet kills Claudius. Gory, dramatic—a long drawn out shuffling off of the mortal coil.

The body count and the violence set against the insanity of our state was just delicious. For a moment I felt OK. I didn't forget that I was dead, but for that span of time, in that circle watching the tragic human spectacle of Hamlet performed by ghosts, I didn't mind being dead—I actually *liked* being dead. This was my first real taste of "acceptance." What it might be like to be OK, to be a ghost, to have friends, to have fun.

It didn't last long; after the play was over, Banquo escorted me back into the mortuary and stood me in front of a door to one of the "rooms." A sign was posted there that said: "In memory of Joseph Jeffery Lynch. Viewing Hours

2 p.m. to 5 p.m. Graveside Memorial Service to follow."

All the warmth that I had gained at the Circle drained out of me, and I felt myself begin to slip away. "Stay with me JJ. You can do this," Banquo said in his deep, reassuring voice. "You are ready for this JJ, this is what you need."

I was split. Part of me wondered who would come. Would Rhiannon make it? How was Nate doing, how was Ma? Just underneath that curiosity was fear—I can't bear to see them broken up about this. What if no one comes, what if no one cares? Maybe my life didn't make a difference. But my ma, I can't bear to see her cry, I just can't. This has to be hard on her, doesn't it?

The room faded away, Banquo faded away, and the faces of my loved ones spun around me. First Ma, grief stricken and crying; then Nate, furious that I had left them; then my sister Jean bored by the subject and ready to move on; then Rhiannon telling me I never meant anything to her and our breakup was the best thing that happened to her.

Faster and faster the voices came—grieving, dismissing, angry, sad, carefree—over and over again. Every emotion painful to watch, every one a blow. I sank down and tried to cover my eyes, but I didn't have eyes, there was nothing to cover. I tried to cover my ears, but I didn't have those either. I was helpless, lost in the swirl of guilt, fear, and recrimination.

I cried out, "I'm sorry, I'm sorry, please leave me alone!" Then I tried to address each one of them: "Don't cry Ma, I'm OK. Nate, please don't be angry with me, it wasn't my fault. Sis, how can you be so heartless? Rhiannon, I loved you, how can you say that to me?"

My pleadings turned to begging, and then to incompressible moaning.

I didn't know it at the time but I was a bardo-brain. I had fully entered Stage #3: Depression, and I was sinking into my own personal hell.

After a time I could not measure, I thought I heard a song from far away. I stopped pleading and tried to listen to it, but the voices got louder and drowned it out, and I sunk back into my fear and guilt infused swim in the bardo. The pain was intense and unrelenting, but I felt I deserved it. I tried to deny what the voices were saying, but their logic was unassailable. I had died. I had failed. I had let people down and caused them pain. I had blown it with the only woman I had really ever loved.

Sometime later I heard the song again. This time it was loud enough for me to understand the words and I recognized it as, *Don't Fear the Reaper*.

The voices of my loved ones got louder, their faces bigger and their emotions more intense, but I moved my attention to the song, focusing on making *it* louder.

I will tell you now, that this is one of the hardest things I have ever done, alive or dead. I could not block out the sounds or sights of the bardo, and still had to focus on the song, making it bigger. I was turning my back on my worst fears, and finding the strength to, at first hum, and then to sing.

It took time, it seemed like a year at least, maybe a century, but the song started to dominate. The lyrics pentrating through my thick scull, slowly drowning out the accusations of my lved ones.

I began to sing louder, and to run, remembering my friend Jesus, my friend Banquo, and the joy of Hamlet performed by ghosts. I sang louder and ran faster until...

Until I found myself running through the gravestones with Banquo and several other ghosts beside me. All of us singing, all of us running.

I stopped and wept. I don't know what it looks like for a ghost to weep, but it felt like I was weeping. The relief of being out of there, of being back in a graveyard, of just being dead was like heaven. It was a joy that is hard to describe.

"Good job boy, good job!" Banquo boomed.

"I knew you would get there, no way we are losing you," Fredrick said, a smile on his face, his form gone wispy around the edges from the effort (which I would come to understand later).

Jim was also there with his cowboy boots and hat, and next to him Jane.

"I... I..." I tried to talk but was overcome and wept more. Nah, I didn't weep, I cried like a baby, I ain't ashamed to admit. A dip in the bardo was enough to make me grateful for what I had: a spectral form and a couple of new friends.

"You are welcome, my boy. You are welcome." Banquo's words were echoed by the others.

As I stood there in the bright sunlight, coming back to my senses, I asked, "How long?"

"Nearly twelve hours," Fredrick answered looking at his pocket watch. Yes, Fredrick had a working pocket watch— a ghost's form can indeed be that detailed with sufficient practice and focus.

"Sorry JJ, but it's time," Banquo said.

I knew what he was talking about, but oddly I felt up to it. Having faced the worst of my fears and surviving my first NBE (Nearly Bardo-ed Experience) I felt ready—well not ready, maybe able—to face my loved ones.

Banquo walked with me back to the mortuary and to my "Viewing Hours."

Interview Transcript
Janet Lynch / Nate Luca: Part 3

Janet: Oh my God! That bardo thing sounds horrible.

Tamara: Can you speak to the story he told about his father?

Janet: What? Oh, yes. We both worked, JJ's father and I—the child care costs were just too much. Once he was in first grade his father would take him to the garage after he got out of school.

Tamara: Anything else?

Janet: Well... He was a good assistant, but it wasn't quite like he explained. He was six, you know, he kept getting distracted and wanting to run around. It took quite a bit out of his father to both work and to try to take care of him. When he was a few years older, he really did become a help. But, I'm...

Tamara: Did you have a question Janet?

Janet: Well, why is my boy in the graveyard in the first place? Why didn't he go to heaven?

Tamara: I'm sorry, I don't know. We are just trying to

determine the accuracy of this document to the best of our ability.

Janet: Accuracy? You can't verify most of this stuff. That strange gathering of dead people, doing Shakespeare and such.

Tamara: No, we can't, but we can verify a lot of the incidents that had witnesses.

Janet: (to Luca) Nate, do you believe this?

Nate: (nodding his head) I do.

Janet: Why?

Nate: (hesitantly) Well, it just sounds like JJ.

Janet: And?

Nate: And what?

Janet: And you are not telling me something. What are you not telling me?

Nate: (sighing) It's coming, I'm sure it's coming.

Transmission #6
Received 2010/10/24 02:10:11

Until I hit my teen years, I spent a lot of time in the garage with Dad. I soon found out that while I had great hands, I lacked some of his other gifts. He was great at finding problems, and also great with the customers.

Once the problem was determined, there was no one better at doing what needed to be done than me. "JJ, you've got the best hands in this place," he would tell me. And at first I felt such a swell of pride, but then as my other deficiencies became apparent I began to feel that I was a disappointment.

I am not sure what that was about. Maybe my talent got all lumped in one area, maybe I was just too impatient. I wasn't good with the customers; I didn't have the patience to gab with them. Dad would say, "They gotta know you before they can trust you, son. And for them to keep coming back, they gotta trust you."

My age, I am sure, was a factor. They would look over my shoulder, not trusting that an eleven- or twelve-year old could do a good job, could work the credit card machine, or could count change correctly.

I was great at the basics, but when a car came in with an odd problem, I had the hardest time tracking it down. Dad would patiently guide me through a nice logical process of elimination, but for some reason I could never do it on my own. He was very patient, guiding me, using clues and diagnostics to slowly reduce the number of things that might be the issue down to just a few. It all made sense, but I just wanted to dive in and get dirty. He would let me do that with junkers, but not customer's cars. And even on the junkers, I would have such a good time pulling it apart that I wouldn't necessarily solve the problem I was after.

I spent time at the garage right up until I left for college, but less and less after the hormones kicked in. There were a couple of reasons for that: Dad and I started to fight—his demanding ways started rubbing me the wrong way; and girls (of course).

And I hate to say this, but we never got past that phase in our relationship. He died before I got old enough to appreciate him again. I've always regretted that.

Transmission #7
Received 2010/10/24 04:12:34

It might seem like a romantic notion to attend one's own funeral, but it's not. How can it go right? If people are holding it together you question your value to them, if they are falling apart you feel guilty about your departure. There is no winning here, no good outcome.

I was beginning to trust Banquo, so when he escorted me in and said, "Stay with it JJ, you can handle this," I wanted to believe him.

"Uhhhh, if you say so Banquo."

"Just stick with it, all of it, and you will be OK." With that he left.

There were lots of folks there. Family: Ma, Jean, Uncle Frank and Aunt Sally, Aunt Ann on my Dad's side of the family, and a smattering of cousins. Friends: college and work, old family friends, and a few from high school. There was also a bunch of older folks I didn't recognize, probably there to support Ma. Last, but not least, was the "meat that once was me" laid out in a coffin at the front of the room with nice flowers and a few picture boards.

Ma looked sharp, dressed all in black. She held it together good, though you could tell from her eyes she had been crying a lot. She was polite to a fault and greeted everyone that came in, shaking their hands and looking in their eyes, thanking them for coming and for their kind words. My sister stayed close, more for her than for Ma, I would think. She didn't look like she had been crying, but had that "deer in the headlights" look, as if she might bolt at any moment.

Mom's brother, Frank, also stuck by her. It was uncharacteristic and touching. Uncle Frank wasn't the most touchy-feely guy you ever met. He was outgoing and boisterous with a wicked sense of humor, but usually ran for the hills when it came to "feelings." But there he was next to her the whole time. It really touched me, so I took my lead from him and just stuck with Ma. I don't know, I guess I was hoping that she would feel my presence and somehow find some comfort with me there. I also knew that I would get a good view of the proceedings—everyone would eventually come and talk to her.

After I settled in, I became aware of this tugging in my gut—something was wrong, something was missing. It took a while, but I finally figured out what it was: Nate and Rhiannon were not there. The two most important non-family relationships I had, and neither one had showed up. It hurt, a lot. I couldn't do anything about it, so I just stuck with Ma, and focused on her, and the people talking to her.

John Denson, my boss at UA, came and said, "A good kid, he was a good kid." He shook Ma's hand and pressed his left hand to her shoulder. He was dressed in a suit that fit poorly and accentuated the roughness of his form. "Hard worker too, I always knew he would follow through on his commitments."

"Thank you so much Mr. Denson, that means a lot," my mom replied.

"That boy," Uncle Frank jumped in, "was always busy. I remember the summer he stayed with me, and I tried to teach him how to fish." He kept doing that, jumping in with small stories, I think he was trying to take the burden of talking off of Ma.

"Sorry, I'm just so sorry. Why..." Mr. Denson trailed off.

"Thank you for coming, I know JJ was fond of you," Ma added.

Mr. Denson shuffled on past and with a pinched look on his face joined the line for the viewing of the meat.

Tam and Jin came. Tam looked stunning in her fitted black skirt and blouse. She always wore loose clothes in the lab; seeing her this way made me wish I had been able to do something about that. She must have had known how I felt about her, but I think we were both too wounded to do anything about it.

"Mrs. Lynch, I am Tamara, this is Jin," Tam said to Ma, "we are so sorry for your loss."

"Thank you," Ma replied. "How did you know JJ?"

"We study at the university, our lab was on JJ's rounds," Jin offered.

Tam shot him a stabbing look and added gently, "JJ was our friend." Ma nodded knowingly. "He often stayed late and helped us with our work—he was so good at building things."

"That's right, that's right, we've met once before, haven't we? You must forgive me. JJ spoke fondly of you both many times. I am sorry I didn't recognize you at first."

"That kid," Uncle Frank interjected, "since he could walk he could take anything apart—and put it back together!"

Most encounters were like this or similar. They shared a number of qualities: 1) Anyone older than forty called me a "kid" or a "boy." It felt strange to me, I was almost thirty; 2) No one ever said anything bad about me. That was weird too. I was far from perfect and screwed up countless times, but today it was like I had never done a thing wrong or spoke a harsh word; 3) No one had anything profound to say. Everything was a variation on "I'm so sorry," "My sincerest condolences," "What a tragedy," "He was too young," etc.

It was an odd ritual, and it became a little numbing after a while. It was like, who are these people talking about? Who is this perfect angel of a boy that God took far too soon? Whoever it was, I didn't recognize him.

Just when I couldn't tolerated it anymore, I saw a pretty, pregnant, petite woman walk in, escorted by a tall lanky man.

At first I didn't recognize her, and then I did a double take and saw that it was Rhiannon. I was flooded with relief she was here, and then I assessed her companion and her condition, and my knees (such as they were) went weak, and my stomach (such as it was) clenched. I felt like I was going to puke, but couldn't. I wanted to run, but was like Jean now, "deer in the headlights" terrified and unable to budge.

Part of me had held out hope all these years that someday we would get back together. Yeah, I know it, I was dead and that hope ended with my life (and in reality long before that). But that was something that hadn't quite sunk in; seeing her made it real. Far too real. Horribly, horribly real.

Interview Transcript
Janet Lynch / Nate Luca: Part 4

Janet: I am sorry, but that whole day is a blur. It sounds like what happened, what I said, but I can't be sure.

Tamara: No problem Janet. I can say for my own part what is recorded of our conversation is accurate. Not exactly what I said, but close.

Janet: I...

Tamara: What is it Janet?

Janet: The calls... God, the calls I had to make. So many people to tell, and with each one I had to tell the story again. It was horrible. Rhiannon was one of the toughest; the poor girl fell apart on the phone.

Tamara: Anything else you would like to add?

Janet: Speaking it aloud over and over. All I wanted to do was ignore it all for a while, but each call made it real, more real, again and again.

Tamara: I'm so sorry.

Transmission #8
Received 2010/10/25 04:16:25

We have come to the point of this where I don't want to continue. Things get ugly; I get ugly. Perhaps it's time to give a little background information. (Hey! You try writing about your life and death honestly—this ain't easy.)

Rhiannon and I met our first year at UA. I had a few girlfriends in high school, but nothing, honestly, that meant much to me—just the call of the hormones. It was exciting and fun, but didn't go beyond that.

Rhiannon was different. So different.

We were in freshmen English together, but I don't think she noticed me there. Later, after we got together, she claimed she had, but she was just probably being nice. English was in one of those big classrooms with tiered seating that held 150 students. Every day I would watch her come in with her friends—a light playful step, brown hair swept up in a bouncing ponytail, an easy laugh, and expressive lips. I had felt attraction before, but this felt different. Not that it wasn't a sexual attraction, it was, there was just another component. Something deeper, something stronger.

I was just a small town kid from Globe, on my own in the big city for the first time. I never got the nerve up to talk to her, I just watched. Nate, who was in the class with me, used to tease me mercilessly about it.

"JJ oh JJ, where for art thou JJ? Deny thy father and refuse thy name!" Nate intoned after class one day as we exited the building—we had been reading Romeo and Juliet.

"Shut up!" I said.

"What's wrong with you Romeo? You never had this problem back in Globe."

"*She* wasn't back in Globe."

"*She's* just a girl." Nate was never very romantic.

"No, she is not."

"Hey!" Nate shouted towards a group of students, one of which was Rhiannon, waving his hand. "Romeo here wants to meet his..." I launched myself and took Nate down. No small feat. Nate was all-state in high school wrestling and outweighed me by at least fifty pounds.

He laughed and had me pinned in ten seconds flat. He rose and bowed toward the now staring group and shouted, "Thank you, thank you!"

Nate and I met on the playground of Globe Junior High in the 7th grade.

Actually it's unfair to call it a playground. It was this small scrap of half asphalted land with two scrawny mesquite trees, secreted behind a group of dull two-story brick buildings. A lot of kids hung out there for lunch or when class was not in session.

Yes, I am digressing further, but it is important. You must understand Rhiannon and Nate to understand what happens next.

I was a scrawny kid, and got picked on a lot. The bullies

and older boys would seek out kids like me and make our lives miserable. Having never been a bully myself, I never quite understood it. I mean, what was in it for them? Scaring kids smaller and younger—what kind of a kick is that? I still don't get it.

I was scrawny, but I was also tough. I put up with it for all of 6th grade, but early on in 7th grade I just broke. Tommy, I don't remember his last name, was shoving me around. Nearly two years older and a lot bigger, he thought it would be easy to mess with me. He shoved me hard, and I fell on the cement ripping a hole in my pants and bloodying my knee. The jeans were new, and I didn't get new jeans that often. I snapped. I yelled and launched myself at him. We both ended up in the principal's office, me with my bloody knee and Tommy with a bloody nose and a black eye.

There was hell to pay at school and at home, but it felt good, real good. I kinda broke through something that day, broke myself open and found another aspect of myself.

I got more respect after that, but kids have short memories. If someone tried to tease me, or call me names, I would confront them—and boy that felt good. Sometimes they would back off and sometimes it would come down to violence; either way was OK with me. I never backed down.

And slowly it evolved. After everyone started leaving me alone, I started defending other kids I knew, and then any old kid. I got to the point where I couldn't help myself; if I was around and some defenseless kid was getting abused, I stepped into the middle.

Now don't go thinking this was an act of heroism, it wasn't. Doing it was a hell of a high, and I got a lot out of it. I went from being a shy introvert to a confident brat. I gained a bit of respect from the other kids, and a lot of self-respect.

My parents hated it; they didn't understand it. They tried yelling, they tried grounding me, they tried making me see the school counselor, but I didn't care.

Over the course of the year, I worked my way through most of the bullies, and had gotten considerably tougher in the process. I lost fights, lots of them, but it really wasn't about winning or losing.

Now I knew who Nate was, he was in my grade, but we were not close, not yet. Nate was a hard guy to get to know.

One day toward the end of the year, I went up against Arty K. Williams. I remember his name because he was a stickler about it, making the teachers include his middle initial when doing roll call. He was a big, overweight, 8th grader, and mean. I walked around the corner and saw him trying to take little Jimmy Smith's lunch money. He had Jimmy pinned to the wall with one hand, and had spilled the contents of his backpack out onto the ground.

"I gotta eat Arty, it's all I got," Jimmy pleaded. "Please!"

"Think I care?" Arty spat. "Hand it over, or face the consequences."

"Arty," I said, slow and even. He knew what I wanted.

He kept his hand on Jimmy and turned to look at me, his beady eyes glaring. "Get lost JJ."

"Why Arty? Are you chicken?" I was pretty reckless—Arty knew about my fighting, the whole school did, but by calling him chicken, I didn't give him a graceful way out.

People seem to have a sixth sense about this stuff, and a crowd was already gathering around us, Nate among them.

"You don't want to do this JJ," Arty said, letting go of Jimmy and turning toward me while Jimmy quickly scrambled out of the way.

"You leave Jimmy alone and we don't have to do anything."

"He *owes* me money, that's all."

"I don't think so."

"Well I do." Arty clenched his meaty hands into fists and moved towards me.

With the dance over, I launched myself at him, but owing to his size he didn't go down. He staggered back a few steps as I bounced off him, landing hard on the asphalt. He pounced on me cracking a rib or two, and started wailing on me. I got a few good blows in, but it was basically over for me. Normally kids our age didn't hurt each other very bad, but this was looking like something else.

Arty was smashing my face with his fist when suddenly someone dragged him off of me. It was Nate. Arty got up, his face red, and it looked like he was going to take a swing at Nate until he saw who it was. Nate was not as big as Arty, but even then he was strong. With his squat build and big shoulders, no one messed with Nate.

Just then the teachers arrived and all three of us got hauled off to the principal's office.

"Man, you just saved my life," I said to Nate as they marched us off.

He shrugged his shoulders and said, "Guess you owe me."

Once it was clear that Nate broke it up, he got to go. Arty got reprimanded, and I got suspended for three weeks; they were getting tired of seeing me in there.

I was sitting outside the principal's office when Ma came storming in. Boy was she mad. But when she took a look at me with one eye swollen shut and blood all over my face, she softened.

She leaned down and gently touched my cheek, "You OK, JJ?"

"Yeah, Ma. Sorry."

"You run off and see the nurse; I'll come get you in a few." She got up and her face changed as she looked at the principal's door. Her jaw set and her eyes became hard as she tore the door open slamming it behind her.

I didn't catch much of what she said, I was heading away as instructed, but I think the principal got the worst beating of the day. I did hear a few bits: "utterly irresponsible," "shocking lack of medical attention," "liability," and "talk to my lawyer."

It was strange, but I felt really safe that day. After "due consideration," (i.e. my mom doing smack-down on the principal), my suspension was decreased to one week, and Arty got a week of suspension too.

When I got back to school I asked Nate why he did it. He thought for a while and said, "Cause you didn't deserve what you were getting."

And that said a lot about Nate. He was this giant of a kid that thought before he spoke, and had this razor sharp sense of justice. A lot of kids thought he was dumb, or slow—and he often paused before speaking—but he wasn't dumb, he just thought before he spoke. An unusual trait for a 7th grader. Hell, that's unusual for just about anyone.

We bonded then and there: Nate had helped me because of his sense of justice, and I helped those little kids out of my own sense of justice (and the thrill of it all). We had something unusual in common; we understood each other.

After that I seemed to get more respect—no one wanted to mess with Nate, even indirectly.

It's not like I didn't get in more fights, I did. When it happened, Nate would just stand by watching placidly, unless he felt someone wasn't getting what they deserved. If that meant stopping the fight before it started, that is what he would do; if that meant pulling me off, he would pull me off; if that meant pulling the other guy off, then that is what he would do.

I can't say I always agreed with him and how he viewed things, but he was a rock, unwavering.

Interview Transcript
Janet Lynch / Nate Luca: Part 5

Janet: Oh the fighting! We tried everything, but he just wouldn't stop. He went through this phase where he would fight about anything. If I served something for dinner he didn't want, he would fight me about it. About doing chores, about doing homework, about anything.

Nate: (chuckling) He was such a scrapper. Yeah, that's how we met. Arty was huge, I think he would have really hurt JJ.

Janet: Thank you for doing that dear.

Nate: My pleasure.

Tamara: So the events described sound accurate?

Janet: Yes.

Nate: Well yeah, but...

Tamara: What?"

Nate: That justice stuff. I never thought about it that way, you know? I didn't know he looked at me like that. Weird. I just always did what I did, I never thought about it much. He makes me sound like....

Janet: Don't be like that, you're a special man.

Nate: I just do what I do, that's all. I'm not special.

Transmission #9
Received 2010/10/26 02:11:23

I grew up in Globe, Arizona, in the 70s and 80s, when it was a grim nowhere kind of a town suffering because of the low copper prices. The mines next door in Miami drove the economy, and when copper prices were down, Globe was down.

These days with China gobbling up all the metal it can get its hands on and with an influx of retirees, Globe is looking up, but back then it was shrinking. People leaving, stores boarded up in the downtown, and few possibilities for a young man.

My dad is the reason I went to college. He wanted a better life for me and started brainwashing me at a young age. College was never a question—I always was going to go.

He would often ask me what I wanted to study at college, what I wanted to be when I grew up. At first I said, "A mechanic just like you, Dad!" But he never liked that answer much. He told me that I was talented, that I could be more, I could do more. I eventually started telling him that I wanted to be a surgeon. It was the only profession I could think of that you got to use your hands all the time. He really liked that answer. It made him happy, but every time I said it what I really thought was, *I really want to be a mechanic like Dad.*

The real problem was I really admired my dad, and he never went to college. He did all right working with his hands. Why did I have to go to college? What could I learn from books and out-of-touch professors that I couldn't learn in the real world getting my hands dirty?

We went rounds with this. My future was one of the things we fought about. We got into it one Saturday when I was in the shop working.

"Opportunity, son, it's about opportunity," he said.

"I want to work with my hands, I want a trade; I don't need college for that."

"What if you want to run your own business? How much do you know about accounting?"

"I don't want that kind of responsibility—"

"What if you get tired of working with your hands? What if you get older and your hands don't work so good anymore?" he said, wringing his hands together.

I was seventeen at that time and my dad was forty-five. "What's wrong with your hands?" I asked.

He shoved them into the pockets of his grease-stained overalls and said, "Nothing. I was speaking hypothetically."

I didn't say a thing for a moment. My dad getting old? That was a new thought. Forty-five wasn't old, was it? My dad was solid, dependable; the thought of his hands—his hands!—failing him was a shock.

There is a moment when our parents become mortal to us. I was old enough then that I had gone through several layers of the humanization of them, but mortal? My dad was mortal? He really wasn't always going to be here?

When I recovered I said, "Look, if there is something—"

"Go pull the starter out of that Chevy, and step on it. You're not getting paid to just stand there and stare."

That was the end of the conversation and the end of our fighting about college (believe me there was plenty left to fight about). After that I just agreed and didn't push it.

Transmission #10
Received 2010/10/26 04:12:52

Back to college, back to Rhiannon. We didn't actually talk until second semester. By some twist of fate, I ended up partnered with her in chem lab.

The first class was about to start and I was seated at the bench studying the syllabus. I noticed her hands first: small hands with slim delicate fingers; expressive hands, tipped with purple nail polish. When I looked up there was a smile on her face, her ponytail bobbing behind her head, her hand outstretched, "Hi, I'm Rhiannon. Guess we're partners."

I was taken a back, "Ahh, Ahh," I stammered, "I'm JJ." I gave up a quick "thank you" that Nate wasn't in this class and that I didn't know anyone, otherwise I might have already been partnered up when she came in.

I thought I had won the lottery or something: I got to spend two days a week, three hours each day with her. I didn't have to rush; I didn't have to make any grand gestures. The first few classes were heaven, until I met Tim, her boyfriend.

Tim was her high school sweetheart, and pre-med just

like she was. How could I compete with that? I decided that knowing her was enough, that I would become her friend, her very good friend.

I found it was easy to be with her, and from being in lab together we went to sitting together for the chem lectures, to sharing notes and studying together. Rhiannon really helped me with the class part, and I helped her with the lab part. Her mind was quick and sharp, my hands were agile and accurate. She grasped the intellectual, I grasped the practical. We made a good team.

I bided my time, grateful to spend any time I could with her. We soon found ourselves hanging out for non-chem reasons and talking as friends talk. When Tim found himself more interested in someone new, I was there to comfort her, to build her back up, to love her. The transition was easy, graceful, natural.

It wasn't without its problems. Introducing her into the Nate-JJ friendship (dare I say bromance) was tricky and difficult for a while. And worse yet, I never got over the feeling that she was out of my league. She was going to be a doctor, an amazing doctor, and I had no idea what I wanted to do—beyond being with her. She was deep and philosophical; I was down-to-earth and practical. She was beautiful, and kind, and graceful; I was just a guy.

We moved in together in the middle of our sophomore year, and stayed together almost through graduation.

Transmission #11
Received 2010/10/27 03:26:11

My world revolved around Rhiannon—and this was something she loved (the attention, the devotion) and hated (the dependency, the neediness). I knew it wasn't perfect, but it was love, real love. I guess that is what I wanted most in life, and since I had found it, my focus was on nurturing it, keeping it. I didn't find direction in school or in other areas of my life because I really didn't care.

This lack of ambition puzzled her, but she accepted it as those in love accept many small things about the object of their love.

Was it codependent? Probably, but so what? That is just some nasty label some overeducated stiffs have slapped on people needing each other. Yeah, I needed her (and I'll admit I probably needed her too much)—so you gotta problem with that?

Little did I know that this wasn't enough for me. I had lost that sense of "self" I had in junior high and high school when I was getting into fights; it had been supplanted by a sense of "us." I went from fearless with a fire burning in me, to fearful about losing this precious thing that defined me.

It all began to unravel soon after the second semester of our senior year started, when my dad had a heart attack and died suddenly. The shock of it left me stumbling through my life, a mere shadow of myself. I just went through the motions. The pain of the loss was so great that hiding was all I could do.

I started drinking, drinking a lot. Rhiannon did her best, she tried to help me, tried to reach me, but at its core she was trying to get me to face the reality of what had happened. And that was the problem, it hurt so much that I couldn't do that, and to protect myself I had to create distance between us.

She was hurt by this and we began fighting. The anger I felt over my dad's death flared up, and I took it all out on her. Being at odds with her compounded my issues—where was the "us" I depended on? Who was I now that we were not getting along?

So I was either drinking to hide from it all, fighting with her, or deep in depression. This went on for most of the semester until one day she asked me to leave.

"I... I can't do this anymore," Rhiannon said, her shoulders slumped, her bright eyes dim.

I had been out drinking, as usual, and said, "What? You can't do what?"

"You need help JJ, and I have tried, but I don't seem to be able to help you."

"Tried!? It's not your father that died. Don't I get some time to grieve?"

"It's been months JJ, you just keep getting worse."

At this point my head was in the fridge rummaging for beer. "Shit! Where's the beer?"

"JJ, please…"

"Please!? Please!! Please what? Please pretend my dad didn't die? Please pretend everything is OK? Well I can't do that."

"I am not asking you…"

"Then what are you asking for?"

"I am asking you to take care of yourself, to get help, to stop drinking so much."

I hated this, I hated being pushed and prodded in areas that were still so tender, so I turned it back around on her, "Do you love me?"

"What?"

"Simple question." I yelled, "DO YOU LOVE ME?"

She paused for a long while, her mouth stretching tight, "Yes I do, but I certainly don't like you right now. You are not the person I fell in love with."

"So, there is someone else then?" I was still on the attack.

"No," she began to cry. "No! There is no one else."

"Then why do you want me to leave?"

"Because, I am afraid." That shocked me. After a moment she continued. "I am afraid for you, that you will hurt yourself. I am afraid for me, that you will hurt me. I just can't take this anymore."

I slumped down to the floor; I couldn't believe this was happening. My dad was gone, and now this? How could I deal with this, how? I was past what I thought I could endure and yet more was being heaped on.

Rhiannon stood there unmoving, her hands clutching her chest like she was cold, despite the heat. "Nate is worried about you too."

That brought me up short, and I felt an anger seething

inside me, "You have been talking to Nate about this, about me?"

"I didn't know what else to do. He barely sees you anymore, he's worried too."

I stood up, my fists clenched. I was horrified that they had been talking about me behind my back. Talking about how badly I was handling this, whispering things they wouldn't dare say in front of me. I remembered how Rhiannon and I bonded over her grief of losing Tim, and then that jealousy mixed with and fueled my anger.

"So it's you and Nate now?" I was tense, coiled.

"What?" She thought for a moment and then added, "Jesus JJ, no. Nothing like that." And then she thought more, her expression turning from fear to anger, "How could you think that!?"

I am ashamed to admit it, but I wanted to hit her. I didn't move; I just stood there clenching my fists, digging my finger nails into my palms. She must have sensed it because she backed up.

"I called Nate when you got home, he is coming to get you." She was trying to protect herself, letting me know that if I did something...

"Of course you did," I spit out at her. I was drunk, and hurt, and angry, and jealous.

We fought more, until Nate came. I said things—worse things—that I wish I could take back. I said things that haunt me to this day.

When Nate arrived, he literally dragged me out of there and put me in his car. As we drove to his place, I ranted and raved, but he took my anger, and fear, and jealousy with a tight-lipped smile and didn't say a thing.

After I sobered up, I realized how close I had come to

hitting Rhiannon, and that scared me so I kept my distance.

I lived with Nate for the rest of the semester. I was still on a self-destruction program, but Nate didn't try to get me to share my feelings or to talk me out of it. He just stood by, hoping it would run its course, just trying to keep me safe.

I stumbled through the motions and managed to, barely, pass all my classes and graduate.

Shortly after was the intervention.

Interview Transcript
Janet Lynch / Nate Luca: Part 6

Janet: That whole thing was so terrible. My husband was gone and my son flailing—I thought I was going to lose him.

Nate: I didn't know all those details, but it sounds right. It's still weird though.

Tamara: What is weird?

Nate: Hearing someone else talk about you. Seeing yourself through their eyes. Creepy.

Janet: I didn't know much of that either. He almost hit her? I don't think that's true. I can't believe that. He fought, he always fought, but he would never hit a woman, he would never hit her.

Tamara: Even under the influence?

Janet: Well... He didn't do it. That is what matters.

Tamara: So does it sound right, like he wrote it?

Janet: (reluctantly) I guess.

Transmission #12
Received 2010/10/28 02:41:25

It was supposed to be a small graduation party for me and Nate: some of my family, some of his, and a few friends.

It looked like a party, but that is not what it turned into. It was this horribly painful circle of people telling me that they loved me, that I had a problem, and that I needed help.

I responded the way I always do when attacked, I fought back. Never being much for defense, I spent most of my words on offense; making it very clear to each one of them exactly how they had contributed to me becoming that man I was that day.

It was ugly. Terrible. Awful.

Nate was there in the circle, but he didn't say a word. His presence a magnet for me, my attention kept getting drawn to him. Just him being there said a lot; it said he thought this was the right thing to do; it said that he thought I had a problem; it said that he thought that I needed help.

So around we went, back and forth for God knows how long until we were all worn out, emotionally spent. They had given it their best and I had deflected, defended, and thrown it back on them. They were about to give up, I saw it in their eyes.

Then my gaze wandered again to Nate, and our eyes locked, and we began our battle. No words passed between us, the struggle was all in our eyes. The minutes ticked by and no one spoke, no one moved, it hardly seemed like anyone breathed.

And then something changed, tears began to well up in Nate's eyes. Nate wasn't much of a crier; I had only seen him cry twice: once when his fifteen-year-old dog died, and once when his grandmother died.

This ran me through, and tears came to me. This was the one thing I could not defend against; he was the one person I could not deny. Another few minutes passed and we both had tears streaming down our faces, but still we hadn't said a word.

Finally Nate broke the silence. He spoke softly, but his words carried a great weight. He said, "Bro, you need help."

I felt something snap inside of me, I took a deep breath and answered him, "I know."

The flood gates opened and I cried. I cried for the loss of my father, I cried for the loss of Rhiannon, I cried for the loss of myself.

They all gathered around and hugged me and kissed me, and let me cry, told me it was OK to cry, that I should let it out. Normally I would have been deathly embarrassed to be seen like that, but I was so far past that, so lost to myself, that I just let it flow. I had no choice, really.

Afterwards I felt weak, like a baby, but better. Then, it became more like a party.

Somehow everyone had forgotten to buy booze, but it was good anyway, for the first time in a long time I didn't *have* to have a drink.

At the end of the night when it was just me and Nate and Ma, she came over, touched me on the shoulder and said, "This is only the first step JJ."

I was shocked, taken aback. I felt like I had just moved mountains, had done more than anyone could be expected to do, and here I was being told it was just the first step. I took a deep breath gearing up for another fight when I caught Nate's eye. His expression was grim and hard, unyielding; it said that he would go the distance, fight me for as long as it took, but I was going to take the next step, and the next step, and the next step.

I let the breath out in a rush, the anger dissipating, and I was left feeling deeply exhausted. "You're right Ma. But..." and this next part was hard to admit, "But I don't know what the next step is."

Nate nodded, almost imperceptibly; he approved.

Ma handed me a card, "Well I do. You have an appointment at 10 a.m. tomorrow morning."

Thus began my tutelage under the great Doctor Romero. She taught me about the five stages of grief, made me—I should say helped me, I wanted to be there—muck around in the deepest darkest recesses of my psyche, helped me slowly face everything I had been hiding from. She was by far the hardest teacher I ever had.

And Ma was right, that night was just the first step, and not the hardest, not by a long shot. It took over a year of intense counseling with Dr. Romero and meds to get me back on track.

By that time Rhiannon was deep into medical school in Texas. She was willing to exchange emails, but that was it.

I apologized, but I never really knew if she forgave me. Our fight was the last time I saw her while I was alive.

Transmission #13
Received 2010/10/28 03:56:10

When she walked into the viewing hours, Rhiannon was smartly dressed in a black skirt and blouse that gave room for the swell of her pregnancy. She still had those small, delicate, expressive hands with purple nail polish, but her hair was shorter, and her face older. Time had not taken away from her beauty, only magnified it; seeing her made my heart ache.

When she saw my ma, she burst into tears, grabbed her, and held her fiercely for a long time. Ma cried too.

Rhiannon's husband—husband!—hung back stiff and awkward; everyone gave Ma and Rhiannon room. They shared a few words, meant for only the two of them, but I was close enough to hear.

"I am so, so sorry," Rhiannon said.

"Thank you for coming Rhiannon, JJ would have..." Ma couldn't say more.

"I always loved him."

"I know. He always loved you."

The embrace ended, and she introduced her husband,

Thomas. They exchanged pleasantries and caught up: she had just finished her residency; Thomas was a doctor too; they had been married for two years; she was due in four months and was excited to become a mother.

I mentioned earlier there are no good outcomes to something like this. Here I was finding out that the only woman I ever loved truly loved me too. A relief? Yes and no.

I was relieved that it all hadn't been in my imagination, that there really had been love. I was also devastated by how I had hurt her, that I wasn't there, that I could never touch her again.

She went to her husband, grabbed his arm, and whispered, "Please stay close, I need you."

Him! She needed him! If I hadn't been so screwed up, that could have been *me* right now. I could be the father of her child. I could be the one whose arm she was hanging on to.

A rage was kindled in me then, a small burning coal. Not enough to engulf me, but a beginning. I was overcome by a need to be near her. I left Ma and followed her.

They spent some time at the picture boards and digital picture frames. She pointed out pictures of herself, shared memories with her husband of me, of her college days.

I was impressed; he was truly graceful about it. He asked questions, encouraging her to talk, creating an opportunity for her to remember. I had to elevate my opinion of him, I doubt that I could have pulled that off so well if I were in his shoes.

She then went to the coffin, letting go of Thomas's arm; he took a step back. It was just Rhiannon and me, and the meat that was once me.

She leaned over and loosened my tie, "You never liked

these did you?" She cracked a smile adding, "I hardly recognize you in a suit."

She paused, tears welling up. "I'm... I..." she stammered.
"Oh hell JJ, I wish it could have been different. I am sorry
it ended the way it did."

She then did something that shocked me. She leaned
down and lightly kissed my corpse's cheek and whispered,
"Goodbye." She was weeping and tears dripped onto my
face as she stood back up.

I am not sure, but I thought I felt something when she
kissed the meat. My cheek, such as it is, felt warmth radiating through it, with a tingly electrical sensation. Almost
as if she had not just kissed the meat, but had kissed me
too. I don't know if it was something I imagined, but I held
to it tightly.

She gestured to Thomas, taking his arm and they moved
off.

I stood there stunned, and cried. I was feeling so many
things. It seemed that the closure I never had gotten with
her had just occurred. A weight that had survived my death
was suddenly lifted. I felt gratitude, deep gratitude, and
watching how Thomas was with her, I knew, without any
doubt, that she was with the right person—even though that
person was not me. There was still an ache regarding her,
but it was minor. Mostly what I felt now about her, about
us, about our time, was love.

The rest of the time passed uneventfully. People came
and went, talked and shared, seeking comfort or closure.
Some finding it, some not. And, at least as far as Rhiannon
was concerned, I did get what I needed. Not what I would
have wanted or asked for, but what I needed: closure.

Transmission #14
Received 2010/10/28 05:24:16

There is no putting this off any more, so I guess we are down to it now. Stage #2: Anger.

We moved on to the grave-side funeral and I was doing fine, floating between my relief regarding Rhiannon and the high of closure. I was seeing the proceedings as beautiful and necessary for both the living and the dead. I felt for a brief moment that I had arrived, I was "there." Acceptance was mine and this death stuff was going to be a breeze from now on. I was so naïve.

It was pretty much your classic grave-side setup. The coffin was there, poised over the hole in the ground, with fresh clumps of sod laid off to the side. About fifteen chairs were setup underneath a rolling sun shield. It shaded the chairs, and misted water in a vain attempt to cool people down.

There was a priest there that I didn't recognize, holding a Bible, dressed in black with a white silk scarf around his neck.

There were a few extra-corporeals there, that hung back

a ways from the meat. I saw Banquo and Jesus. I threw Jesus a thumbs up as I walked by—I was happy for him, he had mastered Lesson #1: Cutting the Cord.

Also wandering around was Marilyn, looking for her cat. She weaved in and out of the corporeals, and stuck her head into my coffin calling over and over, "Motor, Motor, come here kitty."

The ceremony moved along, and I was doing fine. Right up until Nate showed up, that is.

He stumbled over about half way through; unshaved, dressed in a rumpled shirt and dirty jeans. His eyes were swollen from crying, and he was clearly drunk. It shocked me to see him like that, and the rage that had been smoldering leapt back to life.

I went to him, told him everything was OK, that I was OK, but it did no good, he couldn't hear me. He stood there crying as the ceremony continued. Big Nate, strong Nate, solid Nate, stood there weeping and swaying, unsteady on his feet.

Once it was over, Ma came to him. She hugged him, and took her handkerchief and wiped the tears from his cheek. "Nate, you have to be strong," she said. "I am down to one son now, and you have to be strong."

Nate gaped at her, he must of caught what she said; she was calling him her son. Nate wasn't born a Lynch, but he was family to Ma and me.

He swayed and entered her embrace again. He was so much larger than her that she practically disappeared. Sobs wracked his body as he cried—it was nearly silent, and all the more horrifying because of that. His mute tears and convulsing body was harder for me to witness than any wailing I had ever heard.

Everyone walked away and it was just some mortuary suits (Hal and Alice), Banquo and Jesus back a ways, and the two of them there. The suits looked on passively, but didn't do anything. Jesus looked sad, Banquo was inscrutable.

Ma was crying too, the grief wracking her body; the two of them one shaking mass of pain and grief.

The rage grew, took on a life of its own, and began to consume me. Quickly my hands, my legs, my form wisped away and began to take on the form of a hungry fire.

Nate pulled back briefly and said, "It's not fair." Ma nodded her head in ascent as the wracking sobs engulfed them both again.

The rage ignited, and I was completely engulfed, on fire with it. I cried out, an inhuman wail leaping from me. Nate could be mute and contained in this, but I could not, I was exploding with it. My breath was rage, my thoughts were rage, my form was rage, I was rage.

As I wailed a wind came up from nowhere buffeting Nate and Ma. Shocked, they stopped crying and looked around, "JJ?" Ma said.

I wanted to say something, tell her I was right here, that I was all right, but I couldn't—I wasn't all right. This thing was consuming me. My wail intensified, and the wind grew stronger. My rage demanded justice. No, it demanded *vengeance*, someone had to answer for this, someone had to pay. It sought for a target, and quickly found one: the driver of that car that had killed me and his passengers.

His face came to me sharp and clear, his voice a weak pleading for his father to save him. The graveyard faded as his face became clearer and clearer. I heard a sharp snapping sound, and suddenly I wasn't there anymore. I was on a golf course watching my murderer tee off.

My wail and the wind followed me, buffeting my murderer with such force that he nearly fell over. I wanted to cause him pain, I wanted to destroy him, I wanted him to die. The fire that was me, that was my rage, wanted to feed off of him and consume him until there was nothing left.

That burning mass that was now me descended upon him.

Transmission #15
Received 2010/10/29 02:14:53

When the rage took me, I didn't really understand what was happening. Later, as Jesus and I studied with Banquo, what happened became apparent. That snapping sound was my cord being cut, or more like breaking in this case. I had found something that transcended my attachment to the meat: my anger.

My transformation to a flying ball-o-fire was under Banquo's Lesson #2: Appearance Matters. Spirits don't have bodies, but they do have forms. Kinda like an avatar in a virtual environment: it is malleable and changeable. For the most part spirits look like they did when they were alive; it takes energy and practice to maintain another form. This explains why we don't all look like movie stars, or aliens, or monsters, or whatever might appeal.

Just like a kid, a new spirit's emotions show. That is in essence what happened to me. The strength of my feelings overtook me and my form became something that better represented them. In many ways I wasn't JJ anymore. That ball of fire was a much more primitive part of me.

I also stumbled into Lesson #4: Traveling. My total focus on my killer's face brought me to him. Simple really, but achieving that level of focus is not easy, and "traveling" is something I still have not figured out how to do on purpose.

The rage that was me swooped down on my murderer, hitting him as a focused fireball right in his belly and passed right through him. I did have an effect though; he turned three shades of green, and barfed all over himself.

Far short of the death and destruction I was shooting for, but it was a more dramatic effect then I had ever managed. A dim part of me took pleasure in that.

Unfortunately everything that had occurred since I last "faded" (being bardo-brained; viewing hours; my funeral; turning into a rage monster; cutting the cord; transporting myself; and attacking my killer) left me severely depleted. The scene wavered and faded, and there was no more golf course, no more rage, and there was no more me.

Transmission #16
Received 2010/10/29 04:01:12

I was out for a long time, four or five days at least. When I did come back, I came back angry. Nothing like the monster that I briefly was, but I wanted revenge.

I woke in a large apartment with hardwood floors and high ceilings; bright sunlight flowed through large windows. It was beautiful, elegant with brightly painted walls, and had this cool retro look; not the kind of place I could ever afford. There were two bedrooms (one set up as an office with two desks), two bathrooms, an open living room, and a kitchen area.

I looked out one of the windows and recognized the neighborhood: I was in an expensive apartment building just south of the university. It was a two-story structure shaped like a U, an older restored place.

No one was there, but I could tell from the photos and the clothes in the closest who lived there: my killer, and that girl that was with him, the one that was all inconvenienced by me dying.

Looking at the mail piled on the desks, I found out that

his name was William Arthur Reynolds (another middle name obsessive, like that big bully from junior high, Arty K. Williams), and hers was Anna-Beth Smithson.

Also on the desk was a school newspaper article about the accident. I could only read the first few paragraphs, it said:

"Tragic Accident Kills University Employee. Joseph Jeffery Lynch, a 2002 alum and employee of the university was tragically killed on August 22nd, 2010 when the steering system on the car driven by William Arthur Reynolds, a junior in the business school, failed causing the car to swerve..."

I walked away, my anger seething again. That was no steering failure; it looked like "Daddy" took care of things for little Willy. I resolved to take care of Willy and Anna-Beth, and then move on to Daddy.

As I stomped back into the living room I saw Banquo standing there. I stopped short. His mouth was pulled into a frown, his round face sour. We just stood there for a time staring at each other. I finally broke the silence, "What do you want?"

"I want to help you JJ."

I stopped, and thought for a moment. "OK, you can help me." One eyebrow raised, but he didn't say anything so I forged on. "You can teach me. Teach me how to affect meat folk."

He was silent again for a time until he said flatly, "No."

"Why not? You said you wanted to help me. This is the help I need. I know we can do stuff to them—I already have done it myself—but I need to know more. I need to know how to really do it."

Banquo folded his arms, resting them on the shelf of his

belly. His form, as always, was impeccable—well defined and solid looking. I glanced down at my own form, I was a mess: poorly formed limbs tinged with a red hue. As I focused on them they became better shaped, but still quite transparent, and still hued in red.

"You are talented JJ, there is so much you could do here."

"Yeah, so teach me."

"Not while you are like this."

"Like what?"

"You are steeped in anger, you are here for revenge. It is obvious." He was referring to my hue, what he called an "aura."

"It's not fair. That bastard killed me and got off scot-free—steering malfunction my ass!"

"Revenge will bring you nothing, it can't make you live again."

"Yeah, well maybe I'll feel better. Justice must be served."

"So, you liked the bardo that much?"

That shocked me. "What?" I asked.

"You go down this path JJ, and that is where you will end up, the bardo."

I stopped for a moment and tried to think about it, think it through. I couldn't. My mind kept slipping back to what had happened, to what was taken from me, to the image of Ma and Nate wracked with grief next to my grave site.

"I can't stop," I finally said.

"I'm sorry JJ," Banquo said with a sigh, "then I can't help you."

Interview Transcript
Anna-Beth Smithson: Part 1

Subject: Anna-Beth Smithson

Interviewed By: Tamara Watson

Date: 2/10/2011 10 a.m.

Tamara: Ms. Smithson, thank you for agreeing to this meeting.

Anna-Beth: This has to do with Mr. Lynch?

Tamara: Yes.

Anna-Beth: But not about the accident? William thought it was about the car accident; that is why he wouldn't come. I can't talk about the accident.

Tamara: No Ms. Smithson, we want to talk to you about your fall down the stairs.

Anna-Beth: What has that got to do with him? (laughing nervously)

Tamara: I want to read to you a few excerpts from this document, written by Mr. Lynch, and have you comment on the accuracy of its contents.

Anna-Beth: (laughing again) But he died before I took that fall. I don't understand.

Tamara: (after a long pause) I think maybe you do.

Anna-Beth: Excuse me?

Tamara: I'm sorry. Mr. Lynch wrote this after he died. He was there when you fell. The parts of what I want to read to you describe the time he spent in your presence, up to and including your fall.

Anna-Beth: (crossing herself and mumbling) He's not coming back is he?

Tamara: I don't believe so. Can I start reading?

Anna-Beth: (quietly) Yes.

Transmission #17
Received 2010/10/30 03:45:02

Banquo left after that, just "popped" out. It wasn't like a fade, which is a gradual transition, but quick and sharp. That intrigued me. I wondered if that is how I got to the golf course when I was raging.

I spent the rest of the day restlessly prowling through Willy and Anna-Beth's apartment. And when I got sick of that I explored the apartment building. There were about forty apartments on the two floors, most of which looked to be occupied by college students.

I am not sure why, but I didn't want to leave the building. I could try to "pop" to William, but I was afraid to try it without being sure how. But beyond that I just didn't want to leave. I didn't even go outside. I felt compelled to stay.

I was, literally, haunting the building.

I spent my time with William and Anna-Beth when they were there. In fact it got so I knew right when they entered the building and right when they left. When they weren't there I would wander around trying to figure out how to affect people without "fading." Since Banquo wouldn't teach me, I was going to teach myself.

I got to know some of the people that lived there: Maria, Henry, and a few others.

Maria lived on the first floor—she would go out jogging early in the morning while the heat was still tolerable and then come home for a shower before leaving for class. She was beautiful.

And yes, I did watch her. I don't do that kind of thing now, but the state I was in then, I couldn't help myself. Watching a beautiful woman take a shower—how is a boy to resist?

It seemed like it would be so much fun and it kind of was at first. But then I began to feel guilty, which wasn't a great impediment in my wacked-out mental state. And after that I realized that my real problem was that as I watched her I wasn't feeling anything; that really bugged me. I didn't have a body, so the flesh didn't mean much. It was a shocking and harsh realization—life without meat. I didn't have a body, so her body soon lost its thrill. And when the thrill was gone, I stopped doing it.

I watched people a lot during those weeks, and the whole meat-ness of being alive really got repugnant: eating; pissing; taking a crap; sleeping; bathing; brushing teeth; making love; masturbating; working out. All of it, I saw all of it and began to be repelled by all of it. So much of your lives are dedicated to the maintenance of the meat, so much more than I ever realized while alive.

It took about four days to get over being a voyeur, and then I found myself needing to be away from people. There were three places in the building that could work: the boiler/ utility room; the supply closet; and a small attic space.

The boiler/utility room was too "charged." I don't know

how else to say it, but I think all the juice flowing through there made me feel uncomfortable. The supply closet was just gross, so I ended up making the attic space mine. It was at the top of a short eight-sided tower. When I needed to rest, or needed space, that is where I would go. I just felt comfortable there, safe.

During my first night there my killer did not come home. I spent the evening roaming around apartments with people in them.

I knew two things I had done that got reactions from people: scream in their ear; and turn into a rage monster and dive into their belly.

The rage monster wasn't practical, but screaming sure was. So I spent the whole night screaming in people's ears. I found out a few things: the less focused they were, the easier I could affect them; women were more susceptible than men; the madder I was the easier it was; and midnight seemed to give me a bit of a boost.

I never got much more than a shiver and an occasional "what was that?" but I was learning.

Transmission #18
Received 2010/11/29 01:46:12

Sorry to leave you all hanging; I know it has been a very long time since I have been here to work on the story. A lot has been happening, so much. We will get to that in due time, but for now back to JJ the poltergeist.

I was lost. It wasn't as if I didn't know better—I did—but I was doing the only thing I could do. I had lost myself many times in life, most seriously after my dad died, and now I had lost myself in death. Part of me screamed out against what I was doing, but that part wasn't making the decisions.

And William and Anna-Beth were not villains here, as I would eventually come to learn, but normal everyday screw-ups, just like the rest of us. A dim piece of me must have realized that then, but I just *couldn't* care.

The next night little Willy and Anna-Beth came home and I caught the tail end of a conversation William was having with his father.

"Yes sir... I understand. I do know how much my education is costing you, and I really do appreciate it... Yes sir, I will do better... Yes Dad, I *promise*." He hung up with a pained looked on his face, his blue eyes narrow and his nose wrinkled as if he had just eaten garbage. Even in the moment it made me appreciate my old-man; while not perfect, he was not a domineering prick.

"Will?" Ana-Beth asked.

William didn't answer, but collapsed onto the couch as they sat down and ate take-out Chinese and watched some loser of a reality TV show.

I stayed around them the entire night, nursing my rage and screaming in their ears while they watched TV. William was deaf to me, but Anna-Beth jumped a few times. After a few hours of it, she complained of a headache and went to bed.

William switched to sports. Screaming wasn't working so I switched. I focused on my hand, and the flickering red hue that surrounded it. While holding it before me and watching the hue I remembered what he had done to me, how much it had hurt those I loved. The red got intense, and after about thirty minutes of hard concentration my hand leapt into flames.

It didn't look much like a hand anymore, but was a wispy stump with fire licking around the edges. That encouraged me and I redoubled my efforts. I was feeling tired, but pressed on anyway. After another twenty minutes my hand was a roaring blaze, and my hate for this man was blazing in my heart.

I screamed, "I hate you!" and plunged my flaming limb into his belly.

He put his hand to his stomach and his face crunched up. I felt a brief sardonic joy, but then he belched and said, "Ohh, I am never getting food from that place again." He got up and went to the kitchen, and came back with a foaming glass of Alka-Seltzer.

I looked at my hand, but it was gone, my form was retreating and I felt myself fading. I was devastated, all that effort, and all I had given him was indigestion!

Transmission #19
Received 2010/11/30 03:25:16

When I came back it was early afternoon and I was alone in the apartment. I hovered there, for a long time considering my options. I was pretty sure that it was possible for an EC to do something significant in the corporeal world, but I didn't know how.

One night a few months before I died, I was at the lab late with Tam. I was helping her do some work on the SECI Chamber. I didn't understand how it worked, but they had plans, and figuring out how to put it together was easy.

The frame of it was complete and we were mounting panels. Tam was handing me the panels and the bolts and tools while I mounted them into position. We were at it for hours and got to talking about ghosts and what they could do.

"OK, we have several base assumptions," Tam said as she handed me the electric screw driver. "Number one: consciousness exists independent of the physical body; number two: extra-corporeal consciousness is capable of generating and manipulating electromagnetic radiation; number three: a consciousness that can do that can easily create set patterns in this chamber that will be translated into letters and words."

"EM, so you are talking about light, radio waves, that kind of stuff?" I asked.

"Yes, those are all examples. Here, this panel is next, it goes over there." She pointed to the location.

"So you think a ghost can generate light, or radio waves?"

"There is plenty of anecdotal evidence," she said.

"Anecdotal?"

"Non-scientific, not repeatable."

"Like what?" I asked.

"Ghostly apparitions, lights going on and off in an unexplained way, voices, radios turning themselves on, things moving."

"Yeah, but that could be just a load of superstition."

"Yes, it could be, but it's not, not all of it."

She surprised me she said it with such conviction. "Really?" I asked. "Why do you say that?"

"Well…" she hesitated and then said, "the amount of evidence is overwhelming; it can't be all wrong. With this project we are attempting to gather data regarding ECs in a scientific, verifiable, repeatable way."

She handed me another panel. On it was the letter V, an equals symbol, and another symbol composed of a circle and a few dots. "What are these inscriptions for?"

"Those are the instructions. If the extra-corporeal can radiate electromagnetic energy in that shape, in front of the detector, then we will register it as the letter 'V.'"

"Wow, kinda like a keyboard."

Tam smiled, "You got it JJ."

"So, your ghost needs to know how to read and write in English?"

Her smile faded, "Well... yes. We had to keep it simple."

"Seems like long odds to me, a ghost happening to wander in here, figuring this out, and deciding to talk to you."

"We have some ideas about that..." she was getting bummed; I hated that.

"I'm sure it will happen. I tell you what, if I see any ghosts, I will send them over to you."

She laughed. "Thank you JJ."

Remembering that night gave me fuel for thought: First of all, I needed to try Tam and Jin's chamber, and second, I needed to figure out if I could "manipulate" electromagnetic energy—I thought it would be the gateway to getting the power I needed.

I thought quickly about what I had seen wandering around. Henry, the building manager, lived down in 108 and liked to listen to the radio. I shot down there as if my life depended on it and found old Henry listening to NPR and tending the little garden he had in front of one of his windows.

Maybe "old" is unkind. It is like all those people calling me a "kid"—not a fair generalization. OK then, to be specific, Henry was about sixty, which means he was born around 1950. That used to seem like such a big deal, such a long time ago, but not so much now—Jim, back at the cemetery was born in the late 1700s. Now Jim, he's old—his meat lived to be about thirty years old, and he's now about two hundred years dead.

But still, Henry looked old. His hair was white and his

shoulders stooped as if the years of firsthand and second-hand trauma lay heavy upon him. He lived alone, but on his left hand was a silver wedding band. I imagined him as a man who once had ambition, but had lost it all and fell back to this simple life of his after his wife had died.

Henry's radio was an old unit setup on a small table by a recliner with a mirror behind it. I stood there in front of the radio facing the mirror. I could see the form of my hands in front of me, but I could see nothing of me in the mirror. What did that say? That light did not reflect off of my form? Well of course. That is why people don't normally see ghosts.

How to proceed? Radio waves: they have a low frequency, a large wavelength—everything uses them. So, to interfere with this radio broadcast I would need to emit EM radiation at the same frequency the radio was tuned to.

Hmmm, I thought. How the hell would you do that? Hmmm.

I pondered this for a while, and kept "hmmm"ing to myself, and then I had an idea. I can see other ghosts, but I don't have eyes. I can hear them, but I don't have ears. They must be radiating something that I can sense. Maybe some of that is electromagnetic radiation. I can't see myself in the mirror because whatever I am radiating is not in the visible spectrum.

The only way I could think of to control frequency was with sound. Sound is very low frequency, and not EM, but if I am emitting EM when I talk, and that is what other spirits detect (i.e. hear), then if I could "sing" in the right frequency I could interfere with the radio.

I got myself very close to the radio and began humming. For the entire day I hummed, trying to create a steady tone of higher and higher frequency, of higher and higher pitches.

I soon found myself making, what sounded to me, impossibly high frequency noises. If I had been meat and done this, glass would be breaking, and dogs would be howling.

By the end of the day I was exhausted and had achieved no results. Again I was dejected as I felt myself fade away.

Transmission #20
Received 2010/12/01 02:12:56

When I came back it was first light and I was hovering above the bed with William and Anna-Beth asleep below me. Seeing them there so peaceful, so trouble free, just lit the fire of my rage again. Why should they sleep?

I screamed, I yelled, I "punched" them both, to no avail. I was desperate to have some kind of effect. I thought about what I had learned from Tam and remembered lights— ghosts could sometimes turn on lights.

I went to the light switch and passed my pulsing red hand into it wishing, hoping that it would come on. And it did. For a brief flickering moment with my energy and rage, and my focus and determination, the light flickered on.

I felt something too. When I pulled my hand out, it was redder than it had been and sparking with energy. It wasn't an entirely pleasant sensation, but I was delighted. I plunged the other hand in, and the light came on. I felt the feeling, the energy coursing through my hand and up into my arm—a tingling invasive insistence.

I held it for ten seconds; the light strong but flickering.

It became too much and I had to let go, my whole form sparked about me. Power, I was drawing power.

Later as I pondered it I came to the conclusion that I had bridged the circuit with my form, the electricity had passed through me—I had completed the circuit, and in doing so some of that energy bled off and stayed with me.

I kept at this, keeping the light on for as long as I could tolerate. I had kept it on over a minute when Willy muttered, "Who turned on the light?"

"Hmmm?" Anna-Beth muttered, rolling over.

I was delighted, overjoyed. That mixed with my rage and I took my sparking hands and plunged one into William's stomach, the other into Anna-Beth's. William woke up a bit and Anna-Beth sat straight up clutching her abdomen.

"What the?" she cried.

"Hmmm, what is it?" William answered, still drowsy.

"I... My... Did you?"

"What? Anna, you're not making any sense."

"My stomach, it hurts all of the sudden, bad."

"Tums, get some Tums. It's just the stress."

"I guess so." She got up and went to the kitchen. I stayed there trying again and again with William—plunging my hand, with its fading energy into his stomach. I was left exhausted and fading, and all I had accomplished was getting him to wake up and roll over a few times.

Transmission #21
Received 2010/12/02 03:12:45

When I came back, I was in the room again, it was mid-morning and no one was there. I zoomed back down to Henry's apartment to continue my radio experiments.

I changed several things. First I would "charge" myself on a light switch and then do the toning near the radio. I kept going higher and higher, but this didn't do any good.

I am afraid that my charging on his lights drove Henry crazy. As soon as any light came to flickering life while I charged myself Henry would get his tools out to look at the problem. While he was working on one light switch I would go to another.

I felt bad about it because Henry was a good guy. He seemed lonely and a bit odd, but gentle. He would talk to things as he went about his day: Greeting each of his plants by name as he watered them; arguing with the shows on NPR when he didn't agree with them; talking to the light switches as he took them apart as he followed my charging around the room trying to find out what was wrong.

"Now what's wrong with you little fellow," he said as he

unscrewed the light plate. I was already onto a different light and he said, "Oh my, and now you need some attention." We spent the day with him chasing my efforts, trying to figure out what was going on.

But still, I was not interfering with the radio. I was about to give up when I decided to try lower frequencies. Tam would have been proud. I hypothesized that higher frequencies were not working because I was naturally emitting electromagnetic energy at a higher frequency than radio waves, so if I emitted at a lower frequency I would come down the spectrum to radio waves.

Soon I was emitting rumbles that seemed like the earth groaning and I saw something in the mirror—a brief flash of dim light. That shocked me. I filed it away for further thought and continued on. I kept going, lower and lower and I eventually got there.

The station, normally crisp and clear, developed a hint of static. I focused harder, and harder. I felt the results of my last "charge" dissipating, but I just kept pushing. Too low, and the station was fine, too high and there was no effect, the frequency had to be just right.

Once again I got the hint of static to come in and I made the tiniest changes, letting the tone completely take me over, the static growing more intense, until that is all there was.

I was exhausted and overjoyed. Henry was frazzled, having one more problem to look at.

I wasn't quite spent so I wandered about the building participating in my already described voyeuristic tendencies and finished the day in seclusion, resting in the tower.

Transmission #22
Received 2010/12/02 05:13:21

I got through the day without fading, which pleased me. I spent time in the tower planning. I decided to bide my time with my revenge plans. I was learning fast, and decided that I would soon find some way to hurt him. So, for the time being, I would "haunt" them at night making sure they didn't get any rest. It would both weaken him and be a balm for the rage that was still consuming me.

I could feel midnight coming close. It was maybe 11 p.m. and I had roused myself to go down and execute my plan, when "pop" Banquo and Jesus stood before me.

Banquo stood there, his form crisp as usual, with a stern look on his face. His right arm was intertwined with Jesus's left, merged in a strange way. It looked a bit like a double exposure. Jesus looked surprised, and his form was wispy and transparent.

They separated their arms, Banquo's arm quickly going crisp and solid, Jesus's staying ill-defined. Banquo said, "Good evening JJ."

I answered with a sour look.

Jesus said, "Good to see you man, how you doing?"

I smiled, I couldn't help it, I was glad to see him. "I'm OK Jesus. Congratulations on cutting the cord."

"Oh, yeah, thanks." His face turned dark, his mouth forming a frown below his black mustache. "Just in time too. I wasn't doing well surrounded by all those bardo-brainers with no one to talk to. Banquo here talked me through cutting the cord just in time."

"He can be helpful," I said, "when he wants to."

There was an awkward silence that was broken by Banquo, "We have come to invite you to tonight's Midnight Circle."

"Yeah man, it's gonna be good," Jesus interjected. "We are doing Macbeth. It should be great; who can do a better ghost than a ghost?"

I smiled, my memory of my night in the Midnight Circle watching Hamlet was a fond one.

"I..." I began.

"It's OK man, Banquo can pop us back there for the fun, and then pop you back here."

I looked at Banquo, "You would bring me back?"

"Yes, JJ. I only want to help you. It would do you good to get out of here."

As tempting as it was, I knew I couldn't go. The thought of leaving without achieving my goal made me sick. I couldn't let Willy get away with this, I just couldn't. Justice had to be served, and it was up to me to take care of it.

Banquo, who had been watching me closely, must have guessed what was going through my mind. "Can we talk about this, talk about what you are doing?" he said, his face and Jesus's full of concern.

The part of me that was now buried, suppressed, felt

their concern and appreciated it. But the rage, the part of me that was in control, was just angry about it.

"Sure," I said sarcastically. "Teach me Banquo. Teach me how to accomplish my goal, to achieve justice." I was challenging him. Justice was my armor, and with it I felt that I was in the right.

"You don't want justice JJ," Banquo said, "you want revenge. 'In taking revenge, a man is but even with his enemy; but in passing it over, he is superior.'"

"Both will be served," I replied. "He killed me, and got away with it. His inebriation was covered up; they called it 'a failure of the steering system.'" I was seething now, red flames flickering on the edge of my form.

Jesus looked frightened. "Justice is for God to deliver, not you," he said.

As I moved out of the tower I shouted back, "'And if any mischief follow, then thou shalt give life for life, eye for eye, tooth for tooth, hand for hand, foot for foot, burning for burning, wound for wound, stripe for stripe.'" Those years in church memorizing Bible verses had finally paid off. I left energized by rage, and laughing a laugh that if I heard it now would chill my blood.

Transmission #23
Received 2010/12/03 01:59:12

I spent that night keeping Willy and Anna-Beth awake. I would let them drift off, and then turn the light on long enough to rouse them, over and over all night long.

It might sound boring, but I was energized by it. I had finally found a way to affect them without exhausting myself to the point of fading. It was a joy, my manic laughter ringing out each time one of them woke up. It was usually William who hauled himself out of bed cursing. As soon as he got half way to the light switch I let it go off. More cursing. On several occasions he stubbed his toe and cursed yet again. The more he cursed, the happier I got and the more my laughter rang out.

By morning they were exhausted and surly with each other. William called Henry at 6:30 a.m. to complain about the problem.

I spent the rest of the morning prowling about the apartment, watching the residents rise and go about their lives: showering, dressing, eating—the mundane actions that make up a meat life.

And while I was disgusted by it I was also envious. They had what I would never have again. I used that to fuel my rage.

By mid morning I was in Henry's place in front of the mirror. I wanted to see if I could reproduce the spark of light I had seen before.

Henry was out, dealing with the electrical issues that were now plaguing the building, so I could pursue my goal in peace. I would "charge" myself on a light switch, and then "tone" down to a lower vibration.

Having had the experience with the radio, this was actually easier. Light is a higher vibration and exists over a span of the EM spectrum. I say easier, but it was not at all easy.

I eventually got the spark back. I could see a small light in the mirror as I toned/vibrated myself at the right frequency.

After resting and charging again, I found I got back there quicker. So that is what I practiced for the rest of the day. I found I could get to the point where I was emitting that tiny bit of light within a few minutes.

I retired to the tower for the late afternoon and evening, happy with my progress.

That night, my war with William escalated. I went down at about 11 p.m. and found them already asleep with sleeping masks on. Turning on the light was not going to work.

I was desperate to keep them awake, so I charged myself on the light switched and plunged my hand into Anna-Beth's belly. She moaned in her sleep, but did not wake up. I then noticed the bottle of sleeping pills on her night stand. She was drugged; the stomach trick was not going to work either.

I paced around wondering what I could do. Light wasn't

going to work, but maybe sound would. How could I make a lot of noise?

The TV, that's it! I studied the unit, a large wall-mounted flat panel. Unlike lights, this did not have a mechanical switch, but an electronic one. Electricity was always flowing through the unit; I just had to fool it into thinking it had been turned on. Normally you would do this through an infrared remote control or by pressing the power button.

While I thought it would be possible to generate infrared light, it seemed much easier to use my form to jump the connection on the power switch. Unlike the light, I would only have to do that long enough to change the state from off to on. Once it was on it would stay that way.

I focused on my hand, making it solid and strong, and inserted it into the power button on the side of the unit. Sure enough it worked! The TV sprang to life; it was showing some late-night infomercial for a mop.

I then used the same technique on the volume button— using my form to bridge the gap, turning the volume up as loud as it would go.

A few minutes later, William came out of the bedroom groggy and cursing. He grabbed the remote from the couch and turned the TV off. I followed him and waited until he had fallen back asleep and then went out and turned the TV back on. He rose once again cursed, shuffled out and turned it off.

We went through this routine two more times, and then he came out swearing vehemently. He didn't bother with the remote and yanked the power cord out of the wall and marched back into the bedroom.

I followed him, and to my delight saw that he did not put the sleeping mask back on. I let him drop back off and then turned the light on. He swore, got up. He was almost to the light when I removed my sparking hand plunging the room into darkness. This time, as he got back in bed, he remembered to put his mask on.

I searched the apartment looking for other things I could turn on, and came across the blender in the kitchen. I again waited until I was sure he was asleep and then, using the same technique as the TV, turned the blender on. Because it was empty, it whirred with a horrible racket. After a few minutes of this William was there yanking its cord out of the socket. As he turned back towards the bedroom he said, "What the hell is going on!?"

"You killed the wrong guy, little Willy," I replied. He, of course, could not hear me.

He went back to bed, again forgetting to put his mask on, so after he dropped back off I turned the light on. We went through this for the rest of the night; I woke him up at least ten times.

When dawn came, he was a bleary-eyed mess. Anna-Beth wasn't much better, groggy from the drugs she had taken.

They sat in bed for a time talking. Willy told her what had happened.

"Will, we need help," Anna-Beth said.

"It's nothing, the stuff just malfunctioned."

"Malfunctioned! Malfunctioned! The light, the TV, the blender, the food processer, the stereo, the clock radio? Something is going on."

"Henry said half of the building has had weird problems with the lights."

"And the TV? The blender? The food processer? The stereo—"

"I don't know. He just told me that he had had the same problem with his lights when I talked to him yesterday morning."

"Will, something is wrong. Do you think it's—" she stopped herself short.

"Stop it Anna-Beth, not again."

"That poor man. I can still see his body pinned to the jungle gym—"

"Enough!" he shouted at her.

Anna-Beth was silent for a long time, her eyes misting up as if she were about to cry. "Will, we've got that party tonight, and we're both—"

"It'll be OK," William said, his voice going soft as he took her hand, "I promise."

"Everyone is going to be here. It's our first big event of the year. If this weird stuff happens then, I will just be mortified."

"It won't, it won't," he soothed, "I will talk to Henry about this. Hell, I'll even throw him a few bucks so our problems will be his priority."

I left, racing back to the tower to make my plans for the party.

Interview Transcript
Anna-Beth Smithson: Part 2

Tamara: What made you suspect it was Mr. Lynch?

Anna-Beth: Haunting us? That's what you mean right?

Tamara: Yes. Haunting you.

Anna-Beth: I don't know. I was having nightmares about that horrible night, seeing him die over and over again. That combined with all the weirdness going on in the apartment. It just clicked.

Tamara: Can you speak about the abdominal pain, was that really happening?

Anna-Beth: God yes. It was this horrible burning sensation, my stomach would just clench up... (pause) You know, I think that is how I knew.

Tamara: I don't think I understand.

Anna-Beth: That is how I knew it was him, Mr. Lynch. It was like every time he punched me I saw that awful image of him again. The blood... how his body just laid there like a broken doll or something, except it was a person. I had never seen a dead body before.

Tamara: So the events described are accurate?

Anna-Beth: (crying) What? Oh, yeah—that is pretty much how it happened.

Tamara: Ms. Smithson, do you need to take a break?

Anna-Beth: Oh. Thanks. I... I feel so bad about...

Transmission #24
Received 2010/12/04 02:21:54

When I got back to the tower, Jesus was sitting there, on the floor, legs crossed. His form was well defined, if a bit transparent. He sat there placidly, hovering about an inch off the floor. I don't think he intended to hover. As a ghost the floor or the ground doesn't support you, but the convention is to always appear as if it does. This is part of Banquo's Lesson #2: Appearance Matters. Details like that are very difficult to get right.

"How'd—" I started. "Where is Banquo?"

"He's not here; he dropped me off, and will come back by to get me when he gets a chance."

"What are you doing—"

He cut me off, "Nice place."

"Yeah, I like it. I have to get away from the meat sometimes. All that eating, sleeping, and cleaning—meat maintenance is starting to gross me out."

"Yeah, I know what you mean."

It was small talk, but I didn't realize how much I had missed having someone to talk to so I let it continue. "So where have you been?"

"I've been staying at the cemetery. Nice folks; I love the Midnight Circle."

"I did too, the one night I attended." I gestured to his form, "Nice form."

"Thanks man. Banquo's been teaching me. 'Lesson #2: Appearance Matters.'"

"So what did he teach you?" I was still hungry to learn, and since Banquo wouldn't teach me, maybe Jesus would.

"Let me show you one thing. You should be able to manage it. Banquo says you are really talented with your form."

I nodded.

"OK," he continued, "hold out your hand and focus on forming it, make it real crisp."

I held my hand up, it was it's usually wispy, vaguely hand-like self; it began to coalesce as I focused on it, quickly taking the shape of a hand. Slowly with Jesus's coaching it went from something of a sketch to something that looked like a real hand that was a bit transparent.

"All right man," Jesus said, placing his hand palm forward towards me. "Now extend your hand out like this." I did. "Good, now focus on keeping it the way it is, but make it solid.

As we sat there, Jesus's hand became solid in about a minute. Mine took a lot longer—he patiently coached and encouraged me. Once both our hands were solid he said, "Now just hold it solid, hold it there."

I did as he slowly brought his hand forward until it touched mine. I jumped. "What the!"

"Cool, huh?"

"I felt something!" Jesus just grinned and nodded. I

was shocked. It didn't feel exactly like being touched, more like it would feel if your foot was asleep and you poked it. I could tell I was being touched, but it felt diffuse, distant.

I was so excited about this that I completely forgot about everything else. We spent the next few hours practicing this. I got to the point where I could quickly make first one hand, then both hands solid.

At one point I tried shoving my hands into Jesus's, and it worked. He floated back from me for a few feet. It was incredible! I never expected to be able to touch someone else again.

"Thank you, Jesus. So is this why Banquo is so obsessed with form?"

"Partially. It's about control and a sense of self. He says it is real easy to lose yourself here. If you control your form, look like you used to look, it helps keep you balanced, helps keeps you sane."

"And if you don't?"

"Bardo-land or—" he paused, looked nervous and hastily added, "—or other stuff."

"You mean like me?"

"Yeah man," Jesus said nodding his head. "I mean like you."

"So that's why you came today?" And just like that things were back to being serious.

"It is."

I wanted to make him leave, yell at him, but I liked him too much. I thought he deserved a chance. "So say your piece, I've got stuff to do."

Jesus talked for a long time, touching on God, faith, and pieces of his history. It was a long and rich story that I can't do justice to here, but I will summarize it.

Jesus was orphaned when he was ten years old, and through some unfortunate circumstances he had to fend for himself on the streets of Mexico City. At first he survived by begging and stealing, but then fell in with the wrong type and was used as a drug mule for older kids, who in turned worked for some big-time drug dealers. He would deliver the drugs and bring back the money; they gave him food and a place to stay. It was a violent and meager life.

When he was fourteen, a nun, Sister Mary Dominga, found him beat and bleeding in an alley. Some older kids from a rival gang had stolen his drug money before he got it back to his handlers and they had done this to him.

She took him into a cramped orphanage and saw to his physical wounds. Once he healed, she saw to his spiritual wounds. It was a long battle of the wills, but eventually Jesus found God and he found faith.

I sat silent for some minutes after he was done. His face showed the strain of the remembering. I knew his sharing for what it was: an act of courage and friendship; a reaching out.

Part of me was touched, but I still could not turn from the road before me.

"You are a bounty hunter, correct?" I asked.

"Yes, JJ, you know I am."

"Then you serve justice. Can't you understand what I am trying to do here?"

"What, exactly, are you trying to do JJ?"

I just spit it out. Jesus deserved the truth, "He killed me; I am going to kill him."

He paused, taken aback. He had to know what I wanted to do, but speaking it laid it out naked between us. I could see the pain in his face as he shook his head slowly from side to side. He brought his hands together, bowed his head and prayed, "Mother Mary, please be with us now. Be with my friend JJ and I as we speak truth. As we speak of loss and pain, of human emotions—good and bad. May your light shine upon us, may your light guide my words, and may we all find peace in your arms. Amen."

I was stunned. I had spent plenty of time in church—it was mostly Ma dragging me—but I had never felt it like Jesus does. His faith seemed pure, even though he had been through so much.

He looked at me, locking my eyes with his. "Yes, JJ, I do serve justice. I had to find a way after all I had been through, to do something that would help other kids. Help them not to live a life like I did."

"And I am serving justice here too Jesus," I shot back. "Don't you see? He killed me! He hurt Nate, he hurt Ma, he hurt everyone I loved. He is not paying for the crime; he must pay for the crime!" I was shouting and flames licked around the edges of my form.

"I do understand JJ." He said it and the words just hung between us. I expected him to deny my impulse, try to suppress it like Banquo did.

"You do?"

"Yes, I do. I would be surprised if you didn't feel like you do, given the circumstances." He paused, and took a deep breath. "After I had learned my trade, I went out on my own and found my parent's killer—he had never been brought to justice. I told myself it was about justice, but even after all my time with Sister Mary Dominga I still wanted revenge."

He stopped, lost in thought. Finally I asked, "What did you do?"

"I came close. So close." He looked back up at me. "I

brought him in and collected the bounty. I did my job and left him to the courts."

"What happened to him?"

"He was murdered in lockup before he could come to trial—he had many enemies."

We were silent again. It dragged on full and heavy, filling up the tower as minutes ticked by. When I couldn't stand it anymore I said, "So, say what you came here to say Jesus."

"My friend," Jesus began, "this path you are on is not the path of justice. If you kill him, you will become a murderer."

"That's what he did to me—he deserves it."

"Perhaps he does, but as the victim, are you the best one to judge? You are not exactly impartial."

I didn't like that word, "victim." "I am the only one here to judge him—his daddy has gotten him out this. What happened is considered an accident."

"And what of his family?" Jesus asked. "What would his death do to them? Who will be at his grave weeping like your mother and your friend? Can you live with that?"

He almost did it. Almost. I knew how horrible I would feel if I succeeded, but then the vision of Ma and Nate came back to me and the almost extinguished rage swelled back to life. I am not sure what I looked like, but Jesus crossed himself and looked away, his lips moving in a silent prayer.

I noticed that it was night and remembered the party. I flew off to do what I had come here to do.

Jesus followed me and watched me that night. He had a pained look on his face, but he never tried to interfere. I so wish Jesus hadn't been there, hadn't seen what happened next.

Transmission #25
Received 2010/12/05 02:33:15

About a month before I died, I was again working late in Jin and Tamara's lab. The construction of the SECI Chamber was almost complete. I had been thinking about what they had been doing, and had some questions.

"I am curious, how this," I gestured to the chamber, "is being funded? I mean, how did you get people serious about searching for extra-corporeal intelligence?"

Tam and Jin shared a look, and she gestured to Jin who answered, "Well, SECI is not actually what we got most of our funding for. Actually many of our funders don't know of that part at all."

"Then what do they think you are doing?" I asked.

"EM shielding research." Jin leaned down and picked up one of the few remaining panels, and hefted it above his head. It was roughly square and about two feet by two feet. "You see, this stuff is light, easy to work with. Anything else that shields this well weighs ten times what this stuff does."

"Let me guess, the military?"

"Yes sir!" Jin said. "We believe that this can withstand

an EM pulse weapon, and that is how we got our funding."

"EM pulse?" I asked. "Like what is put out by a nuclear detonation?"

"Yes, that is one way to create an EM pulse."

"And the chamber?"

"Phase one is to prove it can block out EM radiation. To do that we have built a small chamber with some very sophisticated EM sensors in it. If we can get past that stage, more money will come our way!"

"And the ECs?"

"It is hardly realistic to expect an EC to just wander by and figure out how to use the chamber," Tam answered. "Once our phase one testing is done, our plan is to find some willing subjects that are near death and tell them about our project."

"Nice! Train them while they are alive." I thought for a moment. "How are you going to find the folks open to this kind of stuff—it's not exactly the easiest subject to broach?"

"We are still working on that," Tamara said with a shrug of her shoulders and a lowering of her eyes. I could tell there was something more that she wasn't telling me, but I knew to bide my time. Some things can't be forced.

Transmission #26
Received 2010/12/05 04:12:15

The party was in full swing when I got there. The apartment was crowded with about forty people, drinks in everyone's hands. The stereo pounded out music while people danced. The flat-screen alternated between undulating abstract images that moved to the music, and live video that was being taken by some of the party goers.

Little Willy and Anna-Beth were in the kitchen at the blender working on making some kind of fruity rum drink. I swooped over and turned the blender on while the lid was off. It spewed orange fluid all over Anna-Beth and all over the kitchen before William yanked the cord.

"Damn thing's been acting up," he said loud enough so those close could hear him over the music. Anna-Beth stabbed a look at him and stomped off to the bedroom.

I followed her—I had been much more effective with her, so without thinking about it, she is who I focused on for the night.

She found a couple in the room lying on the bed making out. She yelled at them to get out, grabbed some clothes from her closet and went into the bathroom locking the door. She filled the sink with water, stripped off her stained clothes and began washing. As she washed, bent low over the sink, she was whispering, the sound of the water making her hard to hear.

I got closer so I could understand what she was saying, "...sorry, OK? It was an accident; I swear it was an accident. Please, please, please just leave us alone." Her hands shook as she continued to throw the water on her face.

Far from evoking compassion, her pleading just drove me on. I glanced about the room, looking for something I could do to further unbalance her. The light was on, but the fan wasn't, so I formed my hand properly and stuck it into the switch. The fan came to life.

Anna-Beth froze for a moment, water dripping from her face, and stood up slowly seeing that the fan switch was still in the off position. I removed my sparking hand and the fan went off.

"Is that you?" she asked, her voice shaking.

I stuck my hand in again making the fan come to life for a second. She backed up and sat down on the toilet, grabbing a towel and covering herself.

"Why are you doing this?"

I wasn't sure how to reply. I made the fan come on for three short bursts, hoping she would get what I was saying.

She was silent for a minute. "One means yes?"

I pulsed the fan once. *Yes.*

"Two means no?"

I pulsed the fan once. *Yes.*

"Three means you can't answer?"

Once again I pulsed the fan once. She was scared, that was clear, but she was also intrigued, just like I was.

"Who are you?" she asked. "Crap, wait. Are you that poor man that got run over?"

Using the fan I answered. *Yes.*

"Can you please leave us alone?"

I pulsed the fan twice. *No.*

"Shit! Shit! Shit!" She was up now drying herself off, pulling her clothes on. "You want to hurt us don't you?"

Yes.

She ripped opened the door, and ran out, her blouse only half buttoned and her hair still damp. She ran out into the party, bumping into people as she rushed to the kitchen. She grabbed William with one hand, and a bottle of rum with another. She pulled him back towards the bathroom taking a large drink from the bottle and coughing.

"What is it, babe? The blender is just on the fritz."

Her face was red, her eyes wild. "Shut up, just come with me."

William, taken aback, followed her into the bathroom. She slammed and locked the door behind them.

"It's him! It's him! He is here."

"Anna-Beth, really," he began calmly, "I don't—".

"Shhh!" She took another swig from the bottle. "He was making the fan go on, with the switch off." Her shaking finger pointed to the switch.

William's lips pursed and his eyes widened as he assessed her appearance, but he said nothing.

"I'm telling the truth!" Still William said nothing. "I can prove it. He does one for yes, two for no." She took a deep breath and another drink. "Are you here?"

I paused, my hand poised at the switch. If I did nothing, William would think she was crazy. If I did something I might scare William too.

The silence stretched out and just as William opened his mouth to say something, I flicked the fan on. *Yes.*

William's eyes widened. "Just... Just something wrong with the switch." He flicked the switch on and off several times, the fan behaved as it should.

"He said he wanted to hurt us Will!"

"Now Anna-Beth—"

"Still don't believe me?" Anger was mixing with her fear. "Then you ask him a question."

William squirmed, but under her gaze he relented, "OK, OK, let me think." His face formed a wicked grin and he said, "Is Anna-Beth crazy?"

No.

He jumped back as if shocked. He probably thought the fan just came to life on its own from time to time, and that had fooled Anna-Beth. The fan coming on twice made that rationalization fall apart.

"You're trying to hurt us, aren't you?" Anna-Beth asked, her voice breaking.

Yes.

She took another pull on the bottle. William then asked, "You mean us well don't you?"

No.

That seemed to convince him; he sunk slowly down onto the toilet, his face white.

"What do we do, Will? What do we do?" Anna-Beth said, her voice hysterical.

"Just give me a minute," William replied. Anna-Beth paced back and forth between the toilet and the door. Finally he said, "We have to leave."

"But he'll just follow us."

I flicked the fan to life. *Yes.*

They both looked startled, as if they had forgotten that I was part of the conversation.

"Shit! Shit! Shit! Shit!" Anna-Beth intoned, taking another drink, her pacing beginning to waver from the alcohol.

I knew they were on the brink, and I wanted to do something to push them over. I also was worried about them leaving the building; I wasn't sure if I could follow. So, not really thinking, I modulated one finger of each hand and plunged them into the wall socket, plugging myself in.

I felt the electricity coursing through my form. It was much more intense than a switch and it took great resolve to stay plugged in. After a few seconds the breaker on the plug threw, making a popping sound.

I was left reeling with my form sparking with more energy than I had experienced before. My intent had been to blow the breaker and plunge the room into darkness, but I forgot that all bathroom outlets have their own breakers to keep people from electrocuting themselves.

My action, nevertheless, had an effect. When the breaker popped, they ripped open the door and ran out into the party, headlong into the mass of dancing people. I followed, the electricity mixing with my rage as I let out a howl.

I was convinced that I couldn't leave the building (after all I had not left since I arrived) so I couldn't let them leave either. This was my only chance, my only chance to avenge myself, my only chance to make up for Ma and Nate.

They plowed through the crowd knocking people over and made it to the door. Out they went running down the hallway.

"No!" I cried, zooming towards them, my form turning to fire as the rage took me. I aimed myself at William and shot forward.

Just as I was about to reach William, just as they were about the reach the steps, William tripped, and I flew over him and plowed into Anna-Beth.

All the energy I had just collected, all the rage and hate and anger that filled me, all of that hit her in her lower back. She was still moving, poised at the edge of the steps, she shook violently for a second and then her legs went out from under her and she tumbled down the stairs. When her body reached the landing her head hit the wood with a sharp crack. She laid there unmoving and limp, her limbs tangled around her.

Transmission #27
Received 2010/12/06 01:45:21

When I was about eight or nine I got a BB gun for Christmas. Just like that kid in "A Christmas Story," I had begged and begged for it. Ma was worried I would hurt myself or someone else (she never said "you'll shoot your eye out," but she was thinking it); Dad thought I was old enough for the responsibility, and encouraged my dream of owning a weapon.

I'm not really sure why I wanted it so badly; a rite of passage of some sort I guess. If I had a gun—even a BB gun—I wasn't a little boy anymore. I was on my way to becoming a man. I could do things, I could defend myself.

When it showed up on Christmas morning, I was overjoyed. It wasn't an "Official Red Ryder Carbine-Action Two-Hundred-Shot Range Model Air Rifle" like in the movie; it was a Daisy 105 Buck air rifle. It had a real wood stock and a steel barrel—it was perfect.

After some dutiful instructions from my dad, and some long looks and deep sighs from my ma, I headed out with my fully loaded weapon and box of extra BBs jangling in my pocket.

Globe had a white Christmas that year, with about an inch of snow on the ground. I headed a few blocks over to a deep cut in the rolling hills where no houses were. The gully was filled with mesquite trees, cat-claw bushes, prickly pear cactus, and weeds.

I found myself a spot behind a big rock and waited for something to shoot at. The time crept by slowly as the moisture from the snow seeped into my clothing and the cold spread through me.

The first thing I saw was a couple of kids up the gully a ways having a snow ball fight. No, that wouldn't do. A shot to the butt wouldn't hurt them much, but it would sure get me into trouble if I was caught.

I was hoping for game. A rabbit or quail, something Ma could cook. Something a man would shoot, something worth shooting.

Soon I grew cold, tired, and hungry, but no rabbits, no quail, no game. The only thing I saw were a few birds pecking around in the snow. Well, if that was all the prey available then a bird it would be.

Soon my wet jeans, hunger, and other discomforts were forgotten and I was taking shots at the birds.

I missed the first, the second, and the third, but I learned a little bit. After each shot they would scatter, but soon they returned. I learned to be patient and let them come close.

Eventually one did. I think it was a robin; it had dull grey feathers with a red/orange breast. I took careful aim and shot. It flapped briefly and fell over in the snow, dead.

I walked over and nudged it with my boot. Underneath it was a small red stain.

That image is still with me: that small bright red stain in the white snow, next to the lifeless body of a robin—that stain caused by the life that I took.

Even then I had something of a grasp of the realities of the world—I knew animals died all the time to feed me—but taking a life myself put me in touch with something unexpected. Something dark. Something scary. Something that made me feel a little ill.

A rite of passage? Yeah, I guess you could call it that. I would like to say that was the last time I took the life of an animal just because I wanted to. It wasn't. This was something that took a while to get out of my system.

And every time I killed something—even when it was game and not just because I wanted to—I felt the same way I did standing over that robin looking at the red stain in the white snow.

That night after she fell and after I came to my senses, I looked at Anna-Beth lying still at the bottom of the stairs in a tumble of oddly placed limbs. I felt that feeling, that fear, that creeping dread in the pit of my stomach. Something had happened, a line had been crossed, and things would never be the same again. Only this time it wasn't just a bird.

Interview Transcript
Anna-Beth Smithson: Part 3

Tamara: When that fan came on how did you know it was Mr. Lynch?

Anna-Beth: I just knew. I've always been a little physic—I know someone is calling before the phone rings, stuff like that.

Tamara: So he really did communicate to you using the bathroom fan.

Anna-Beth: I have never been so scared in my life.

Tamara: So he did?

Anna-Beth: Yes. Yes! Jesus H. Christ, yes!

Tamara: What else can you tell me about that communication?

Anna-Beth: Besides learning that my worst fears were true, and a pissed off, crazy ghost was communicating to me using a bathroom fan, telling me he wanted to hurt me?

Tamara: I am just being thorough, is there anything you can add?

Anna-Beth: I... I saw him.

Tamara: Saw him?

Anna-Beth: When he did that electrical thingy, plugging himself in. I saw him.

Tamara: Can you describe what you saw?

Anna-Beth: Even though the light was on, for a few seconds I saw this flickering outline of a man—his hand near the outlet. William saw him too. I screamed and we both ran.

Tamara: Interesting. Can you describe your fall?

Anna-Beth: Like he said, it felt like I had been shocked, my legs turned to jelly and that is all I can remember.

Transmission #28
Received 2010/12/06 03:12:16

I would like to say that I saw the error of my ways right then and there and that I rushed right to Anna-Beth to see if she was alive.

But that is not what I did. Most of the energy had dissipated, but my rage had not. William was lying there befuddled trying to get up. I plunged my fist into him again and again as he tried to move.

I don't think it had much of an effect; he staggered as he got up, but it was probably from the blow he had taken to his head when he fell—I could see a blossoming bruise on his temple.

I was incoherent with the rage, unintelligible noises escaping from me like a beast. As William finally rose, unsteady on his feet, I too stood up exhausted and spent.

I looked down the hall and saw Jesus there, tears on his cheeks (even as ghosts, our forms often mirror our emotions). Behind him several party goers were rushing down the hallway to see what had happened. Then I remembered her, remembered what I had done. I flew down to the landing. She was on her back, one arm twisted under her, blood beginning to matt her blond hair.

It was like waking up only to realize you have already walked over the cliff and are plunging to your death. The bardo came to me, but I pushed it away by focusing on Anna-Beth and making her my world. I looked at her neck, and saw an artery pulsing there, I watched her chest rise and fall the tiniest amount—she was alive! And this was my salvation—if she survived. She must survive, I needed her to survive. I knew the bardo, or worse awaited me if she didn't.

I wracked my brain, trying to think of how I could help her. I looked up to the top of the stairs. There was someone talking on a phone, "...she fell down the stairs, it looks real bad."

"Get Banquo!" I screamed to Jesus.

He shook his head, "I don't know how!"

"Just do it! Please!" I shouted, and turned my attention back to Anna-Beth.

What could I do to help her, what could I do? I just sat there feeling the weight of my actions compound the sinking feeling of dread and helplessness.

William and another woman had made their way down to the landing. "Oh my God!" he muttered, leaning down as if to hold her.

"No Will!" shouted the woman. "Don't move her, if she has a neck injury you could kill her."

I had veered sharply into Stage #3: Deals. I wasn't all that concerned about being dead anymore, I just wanted to stay out of bardo/hell.

I saw what I had done as evil. Not knowing what to do, I prayed. "OK, I screwed up. God did I screw up. Anyone would have been angry! Just please, please, let this woman live. I'll do anything, anything!"

As I ended my prayer I thought I heard Anna-Beth moan. It sounded distant, but it sounded like her. I looked at her, but she wasn't moving. I heard the moan again.

What's going on? I kept my attention on her and tuned everything else out. Soon the paramedics arrived, immobilizing her neck, putting her on a back board, taking her down the stairs to a gurney, loading the gurney into the ambulance.

I just stayed with her, focused on her. Once the ambulance tore off I heard the moaning, more distinct this time, but still her lips had not moved. Soon I saw her head rise. Well, not her meat head, but her spirit head. It slowly began to rise, separating out of her body.

I panicked, and without thinking it through, I pushed her head back down into her body. I am not sure how I did it that fast, but my hands were strong and firm when they needed to be and it worked.

The paramedics worked on her, the ambulance tore through the streets of Tucson, but none of this registered much with me. I just stayed right by her head, my focus tight, listening and watching.

From the ambulance into the ER. From the ER into surgery. Her spirit would come around from time to time, her spirit-head rising. Each time I would make my hands firm and gently push her head back down.

Looking at her face so intently I began to see things that I hadn't before: the regal cheek bones, and thin lips; the high forehead and golden blond hair; the tightness around her eyes; and the slight crink in her nose. She went from a caricature of the spoiled rich kid to a person: a flawed mix of beauty and fear, courage and cowardice. Her face became my world, and I felt my heart open to her.

I began talking to her. "It's not your time Anna-Beth, you have to stay where you are. The doctors are working on you, you're gonna be alright. You have to be strong Anna-Beth, you can do this."

As they were drilling into her head during surgery, she flat-lined. It was like my own heart had stopped, I was so scared. When it happened, her form rose from her body, and there was nothing I could do to keep it there. The force of her rising brought us both up above the action looking down on her body, the doctors rushing below us, shocking her heart, trying to resuscitate her.

She looked at me and said, "I know you."

"I'm so sorry," I said, and I meant it.

"You did this to me, didn't you?"

"Yes." I had to take responsibility. "Please, just go back in, they can save you."

"Why? Why did you do this to me?"

"I was so angry. William was drunk when he drove into me." She looked like she was about to speak, but I cut her off. "I was there; I saw you after you got out of the car."

She nodded her head up and down agreeing and said, "I'm sorry."

"Look, if you want to make it up to me, then just survive."

She gazed down at her body, "So what is wrong with me?"

"Broken arm, broken ribs, punctured lung, bruises, brain hemorrhage."

"Eww, sounds bad. I don't know if I want to go back, doesn't seem so bad here."

"Please. If not for me, do it for William, for your family." I wanted to say more, but couldn't.

"You were haunting us weren't you?"

"Yes."

"You scared the hell out of me!"

"I'm so sorry. Please just—"

"Is this it? Is this the afterlife?"

I had to laugh. "Hell if I know. I haven't been here long. Banquo, the one person I have met that seems to know what is going on, has only said that there is more, but I don't have any details."

Below, Anna-Beth's body convulsed as they shocked her heart again. The beep-beep of the heart monitor started, and her spirit form was sucked back down into her body.

Interview Transcript
Anna-Beth Smithson: Part 4

Tamara: Do you remember the conversation you had with Mr. Lynch?

Anna-Beth: (long pause) He said those things about me? About my face? About my beauty, my courage, and my cowardice?

Tamara: Yes.

Anna-Beth: I... I... I don't understand. How he is trying to kill us one moment and trying to save me the next.

Tamara: He was really a good man; I think he was just lost. His death was so sudden, a horrible shock.

Anna-Beth: You knew him?

Tamara: Yes.

Anna-Beth: When he was alive?

Tamara: Yes, he was my friend.

Anna-Beth: (tears in her eyes) I am so sorry about... about what happened to him.

Tamara: Thank you.

Anna-Beth: You must hate me.

Tamara: (pause) I did. But this, these words, changed

that. They change everything.

Anna-Beth: (rising and embracing Tamara) I'm so sorry.

Tamara: Can we go back to the conversion that Mr. Lynch described while you were in surgery?

Anna-Beth: OK.

Tamara: What do you remember?

Anna-Beth: It's like a dream in bits and pieces. I remember seeing my face and the doctors. I remember talking to the skinny guy with short brown hair and really intense eyes—blue-grey, I think. I remember talking to him, but not the words really.

Tamara: So basically what is described here?

Anna-Beth: I don't remember the words, but yeah—something like that. I remember being so relieved that he wasn't going to try to hurt me or Will anymore.

Transmission #29
Received 2010/12/06 04:32:34

In retrospect, what happened to me seemed like a sudden change: going from being a poltergeist to trying to be an angel. And it was abrupt, very abrupt—it was like the line between sleeping and waking. You can be in the middle of a horrid dream, completely lost to your normal self and them bam! You wake up and your world is back. You are still left with the remnants of that dream, and sometimes that can leave a lot to deal with, but you are yourself again. What happened when I injured Anna-Beth was like that. I woke up suddenly and had to deal with the mess my "dreaming" self had made.

After the surgery, I found myself in an ICU room with William. He stayed by her, talking to her, often holding her hand. The bruise on his forehead had gotten bigger and uglier; he looked drained.

I stayed there too, doing what I could. I prayed, such as I do, for her recovery. Fully in deal-making mode and full of guilt for my actions, I was willing to trade pretty much anything for her recovery.

You know how that usually goes: "Just get me out of this ticket, and I swear I will never speed again"; "Just let me survive this layoff and I'll never play games at work again." If your aim is met, then the promise is quickly forgotten as your life springs back to its normal shape.

The kind of deal-making I was doing was on a very different level. This was life and death. My experience was more like the addict finally and truly hitting rock bottom. I was desperate for redemption and willing to pay a mighty price for it.

Shortly after Anna-Beth was settled in the ICU room, William at her side, Banquo and Jesus showed up. I was by her head; they stood at the foot of her bed.

"You look better," Banquo intoned.

I wasn't sure what he meant, but then I looked at my hands, and the red hue that had long plagued me was gone. "Listen Banquo, I—"

He held up is hand, "No need boy. You made it through, that is what counts."

"But Anna-Beth! I couldn't bear it if she died."

Banquo shrugged, "Dying is not so bad, eh? Either way we can help her."

"Please, just tell me how I can keep her alive."

"I'm sorry JJ, but that is not up to us. If it is her time, we cannot force her to stay alive."

"So what? We do nothing! Can you skip the crap for once and just tell me what to do?"

He was startled, his eyes narrowing as he watched me. For a moment I was afraid I had gone too far. He moved around the bed and stood next to me. "Very well."

He placed his hands near my head and asked, "Feel that?" I felt a subtle sense of warmth enter my head, and spread through my body, bringing with it peace. "Do that. Hold your hands near her wound."

I moved my hands into the bed right below her head wound. "Now what?"

"Focus. Focus on her color improving, on her breath deepening, on her body growing stronger."

I once again focused on her face, trying to pour into her everything that I could.

"No! No!" Banquo boomed. "Don't force it. You do that, and you will fade in no time."

"What then?"

"Gentle, my boy, gentle. Slow. Easy." I tried to relax into it. "That's better, but relax more."

He coached me for a time, guiding me to let go more and more. Once again her face became my world and soon I felt the warmth moving through my hands into her. This wasn't the loud, violent energy of my rage, but something soft and subtle. If you didn't know what was going on you could easily miss it.

"Very good JJ. Just keep that up. If there is anything you can do to help her, this is it."

Things happened around me: William being replaced by Anna-Beth's parents; doctors and nurses coming and going; machines beeping and people moving about. None of that mattered to me; all that I cared about was the warmth in my hands and that face. Soon I could have counted every hair in her eyebrows, every eyelash, and every pore on her nose. I don't think I have ever known a face that well before.

And that warmth was there—after a long time with it I found a name for it: love. Not like a man loves a woman, or a mother loves her child, but a different, more elemental, kind of love. More like how the river loves the land, or how the sun loves the moon. I wasn't praying anymore, or making deals anymore, or even thinking about the future anymore. I was just in that flow, that love, with her.

Soon the motions around us sped up into a blur. We were running at a different pace—as people and time whirled around us. Days passed in what seemed like minutes until finally Anna-Beth woke up.

Transmission #30
Received 2010/12/07 02:12:45

At some point, in the blur, they had removed her breathing tube. She took a deep breath, and her eyes popped open.

William was there, holding her hand as he slept, his head leaning on the bed, his breathing deep.

"Wiilllll," Anna-Beth croaked. William jerked to consciousness and looked at her.

"You. Look. Like. Shit." Her words came out slow and weak, but understandable.

"Thank God!" William said as tears formed in his eyes. His face turned dark and he added, "That ghost did this, what are we going to do?"

"It is OK. Will leave alone now," Anna-Beth said, her voice getting steadier.

"He'll leave us alone? How do you know? Did you see him?"

She nodded.

William slumped in palpable relief.

"Must. Make. Amends." William and I were both shocked by this. He stiffened, his eyes frightened. "For what we did," she added.

Relief flooded through me. She had lived. She wanted to make up for what had happened to me. The relief was a letting go, and I felt the weight of what I had been through recently lift. The scene faded rapidly, and I knew nothing else for quite some time.

Transmission #31
Received 2010/12/07 03:34:12

I didn't really put this together while I was alive, but I was using the same kind of strategies with Tamara that I used with Rhiannon. I was working on the slow and careful transition from friendly, to friends, to maybe something more. I am something of an acquired taste. Intimate relationships work better for me if they are given time to grow slowly.

I wasn't really conscious of what I was doing, I just liked her and enjoyed being with her. I wasn't ready for anything more than a casual relationship, and she didn't appear to be ready for any kind of relationship. Besides, I knew it couldn't be just casual with her.

She had this wound, this secret, that drove her to do the SECI project and I really wanted to know what it was. I had a feeling that it was important and essential to understanding her, and I wanted to understand her. I didn't pry or push, I just patiently waited for my opportunity.

I had been running into her for a few months at this little Italian café on campus that had great coffee. OK, most of the "running into her" was intentional; she often got cappuccino in the late afternoon and I just happened to come by when she was there a few times a week. Part of the strategy, you know. It is important to extend the friendship beyond the initial, limited venue. For Rhiannon it was chem lab, for Tamara it was her and Jin's lab.

The conversation that day started innocently enough, I was going on about the Mustang that Nate and I were fixing up and she looked wistful and said, "John loved Mustangs."

"John," I asked, "who's John?"

"He..." she paused and I could see the wheels turning. This was an intimacy she was about to share. "He was my fiancé?"

"I didn't know you had a fiancé... Wait, *was*? What happened?"

"He died," she said in a flat even tone.

"I'm so sorry," I said.

"Thank you JJ."

That was the end of the conversation, she excused herself and left. That got me thinking about her and SECI; it wasn't a hard leap to make: a dead fiancé and a driving need to talk to the dead. There was a story there for sure.

Transmission #32
Received 2010/12/07 04:50:12

When I came to, I was staring at a small plaque in the ground: "Joseph Jeffery Lynch. November 5, 1980—August 22, 2010." I was back in the graveyard, hovering over my own grave. I rushed away; I didn't feel comfortable there.

Before long, I ran into Jesus. He told me I had faded for a full six days. Some had been worried that something had happened to me, but Banquo had told everyone that I must have made amends and moved on.

For the next week or so, I entered into a hybrid state of Denial and Acceptance. I was accepting my death, and no longer sought justice or vengeance, but there was a nagging unease that I was happy to deny.

I spent most of my time with Jesus. We hung around the mortuary, greeting new arrivals, and tried to help the bardo-brains; we went to the Midnight Circle; and took lessons from Banquo when he would give them.

He would usually come around in the morning, and lecture us on Lesson #2: Appearance Matters. Jesus was way ahead of me and I had some catching up to do. We would watch out for each other's form to keep ourselves on track.

To be honest, I didn't care that much about form. I wanted to go on to some of the other lessons, particularly "Traveling," and I wanted to talk about what I had done when I was raging. But Banquo would hear nothing of it; he insisted that unless we mastered our form, then the rest wasn't worth teaching us.

And I've got to tell you, holding a crisp, solid form is not an easy task. I began to admire Banquo with his suit and tie—that is a lot of detail. I settled on blue jeans, a long sleeve black t-shirt, and brown hiking shoes. If I was feeling cocky or felt the need to "dress up" I would add a navy blue jacket. Jesus also went with jeans and a t-shirt, but with cowboy boots.

I eventually switched shoes, I had to. The shoe laces kept tripping me up, as it were. It's a lot of detail to maintain when you are new to this. So I ended up keeping the shoes the way they were, and just ditching the laces—it's not as if I was in danger of falling out of them.

After about three days I was happy with my form, but Banquo was not—"Not solid enough, I can see right through you!" He would not be swayed.

Being a ghost gets boring. What do you do with your time? I mean, what do you do? You can't read, can't write, can't talk on the phone, can't surf the net, don't have to do all the meat maintenance. In some ways it is like taking a step back in time. All the information you convey, all communication, is verbal. You can't write it down, you can only speak it.

Besides being bored, I was restless—my mind kept going to Anna-Beth. So, after Banquo left, I asked Jesus, "Want to go for a hike?"

"Sure," he said. "Where?"

"Anna-Beth, she is only about four miles from here."

He looked at me close, his eyes tight, "Why?"

"Hey! I am over that rage stuff, see—no red aura. I just want to make sure she's OK."

"It would be nice not to sit around here all day. How do we get there?"

"I know the way. Let's fly! We can get a leg up on traveling."

So we set off. We floated up, and headed southeast out of the cemetery. Just like everything else these days "flying" took some practice.

At first we were real slow, maybe one mile per hour, but over the next few days we got so we could do it in ten minutes. Today it took us about three hours.

We found Anna-Beth propped up in bed talking on the phone, "...my vision is still so screwed up, but at least I am still alive."

We didn't stay long. I was tempted to try to talk to her, but quickly discarded the idea.

On the way out I asked Jesus, "Wanna go to a movie?"

"Wow, that would be cool."

"I know this theater; it is practically on our way back."

We got there just as some sappy chick-flick was starting. Not my normal choice, the action flick playing required 3D glasses, and we didn't want to wait around for a better 2D movie. Besides it was free and we needed the distraction.

We settled into a pattern for the next week: morning lessons with Banquo; flying over to check on Anna-Beth; an afternoon movie; back to the morgue for the sunset meet-and-greet; and ending with the Midnight Circle.

Anna-Beth's progress was slow, but steady. It did my

heart good to see that face, and soon it became the high-light of my day. Jesus and I were also progressing slowly but steadily with our forms and our flying.

It was a pleasant week, but there was still something nagging me, still something upsetting me. Once, after one of my childhood fights, I ended up with a floater on the edge of my vision. It caused me such problems; I would try to look at it, but could never quite see it. This nagging feeling was like that; whenever I tried to identify what it was, it moved out of the way. This was really starting to get to me.

Transmission #33
Received 2010/12/08 01:16:21

Even though it is generally frowned upon, denial has its uses: it gave me a week of rest, and time to find a normalcy in being dead. It was a gift, and I was sad when it was over. It was the Midnight Circle that did it. We weren't doing a play; we were just sitting around talking, telling stories of our past.

Although Banquo always lead the theatrical productions, he never contributed to these kinds of stories. Jesus and I didn't contribute either, we were specifically asked not to. They had a rule, not until you were one year dead could you tell stories of your meat-life in the Circle. Something about it being too soon; young ghosts being too fragile. He never admitted it, but I bet Banquo made the rule up.

Fredrick stood up and told a gruesome tale of a funeral gone wrong. After he had embalmed a young man, he caught the man's wife back in the embalming room, both her and the body, in what he called "an advanced state of undress."

Later during the viewing hours the inebriated wife careened into the casket, knocking it over, the body rolling out and its hand slapping down on the ankle of the dead man's mother. His mother screamed, sprinted into a closed door, and was knocked unconscious.

While everyone was busy with the mother, the wife again proceeded to undress her dead husband and herself.

Marilyn told a story about her mother. Midnight Circle was about the only time she seemed sane. She would be looking for her cat all night, settle down and participate in the Circle and then go back to looking for her cat.

The story she told was simple, it was about the pet store her mother owned when she was a girl. Marilyn started spending time there as soon as she was born, and started helping out at about eight years old. "My mother was a born matchmaker; she could size up someone coming in and guide them to the right animal. She wasn't overt about it; she would gently nudge them—'Hmmm, you look like a Yorkie person,' 'Did you see that darling tabby over here?', 'Those labs can be kind of rambunctious, is your household setup for that?'—most people didn't even know what she was doing.

"One night, when I was about eleven, this old man came in with these sad droopy eyes and brown hair. I thought to myself, 'he looks like a beagle.' My mother was busy in the back, so I helped him out. He was dead set on a poodle. He and his wife always had poodles, and now that she was gone, he wanted a poodle too.

"He spent almost an hour with the three poodle pups we had, but I could tell it wasn't a match. So, I marched over and grabbed the beagle pup, and you should have seen him! That pup crawled right in his lap, and licked his face; he was delighted.

"He took that beagle home, and was a regular for the next

few years—he loved that dog, named him Nathan as I recall.

"My mother was so proud of me, she said, 'Marilyn, you've got the gift!' That was the happiest moment in my life up until then."

On and on the stories went, and over and over mothers were mentioned. Jim talked about how his mother had died on the way across country to Arizona. Adriana, the old gypsy, mentioned the curse her mother-in-law had placed on her, leading to her own death. Little Anton spoke of the pancakes his mother used to make him every Saturday morning.

It seemed like it was staged, planned. Everyone had conspired to talk about their mothers for my benefit. I felt the space closing in around me. Fredrick was starting a story about how he had to embalm his own mother when I snapped.

"Enough!" I shouted.

Everyone was shocked, I was shocked, I hadn't meant to say that out loud. The Circle went silent, everyone staring at me.

"Sorry Fredrick. Ummm. I don't feel well." Embarrassed I slunk way.

Jesus followed. "What's up man?"

"I finally figured out what has been bugging me. My ma, I have got to make sure she is alright."

Jesus shrugged, and said, "OK, let's go see her."

It was an obvious solution to me, but a surprise. After my going off the rails with William and Anna-Beth, I had let my life get small.

"Anna-Beth is doing well," he continued, "and we don't have to stay here."

I smiled, heartened by his offer. "OK then, off to Globe we go."

Globe is about one hundred miles north of Tucson. We flew, sticking to the road so we didn't get lost, and got there just as the sun was rising.

Transmission #34
Received 2010/12/08 02:22:12

Even in town, Globe has a rural feel. The influx of retirees has changed that some, but not much: cowboy boots, cowboy hats, chewing tobacco, the whole western thing.

I've always described the area as a "hilly desert." The elevation there is higher than Tucson and Phoenix, and it is usually about ten degrees cooler. The Pinal Mountains are nearby, as well as Lake Roosevelt.

My house, where I was born, and Ma still lived, was just up the hill from the high school on Mesquite. It was a little white house that had been turned into a duplex, and then back into a house when my parents bought it.

Jesus and I landed on the scrap of a front yard just after dawn, a "For Sale" sign in the yard.

I was upset and stormed through the house, everything was gone, and no one was there. I came back out and "sat" on the landing—more form practice, it was becoming a habit; sitting in a natural way is tough when nothing presses against you.

I sighed, "She's gone." I thought I saw a flash of movement

down the street, but when I turned my head, it was gone.

"No problem my friend, this is my area," Jesus said as he walked through the door. I got up and followed. "I find people, remember."

We meticulously walked the house and the property, but didn't find anything useful—Ma had cleaned the place good. Jesus said he would normally go through the trash, or talk to the neighbors, but that wasn't possible for us. After about half an hour we both "sat" on the landing.

"OK, no problem, we'll find her," Jesus said. I was feeling dejected and didn't reply. "Did your mom work?"

"She was a court recorder down at the court house. Been doing it for about thirty years."

He stood up and looked at me, I hadn't moved.

"Well, let's go. She might be there."

We got up and walked down to the street. On our trip up we had agreed to spend the day practicing our "walking." We knew it was the next skill that Banquo would demand of us before teaching us more. Just like sitting, walking is strange without a body. It's kind of like making a marionette look natural while sitting or walking—it isn't natural and it's hard to do.

Because we were paying attention to our "walking" we didn't see him right away. He was a big ghost, poorly formed and wispy, standing in the street staring at us. We were both surprised, stopping in our tracks, and stared back.

His arms, such as they were, were crossed. He was about seven feet tall and broad. "What have we here?" he asked.

This pulled me out of my funk; he was a bully. I hadn't had to fight for a long time, but I remembered what it felt like. I became more alert, tense, and scanned the surroundings for his backup.

When we didn't say anything, he continued. "You two will be coming with me. Spencer wants to see you." He gestured and floated a few feet down the street. As his left hand waved in our direction I noticed that he was missing a pinky. I thought it was odd, but didn't think much of it at the time.

Jesus looked at me, and I shook my head "no." We still didn't move or speak. I was furiously trying to figure out how you fight without a body.

He came back. "Look, you two are new to town, so I'll cut you a break." His tone was snide and condescending. "Come see Spencer, settle up with him, and you can go on your way."

"Settle up?" I asked.

"You know, give him a donation."

"A what?" I had no idea what he was talking about. What kind of donation could a ghost make?

"You two are really new, aren't you? Noobs fresh out of the grave." He paused. "You will come along, either the easy way or the hard way. You choose."

I felt the rage building in me, just like back in junior high. I caught Jesus's eye and indicated that he should step back. I squared myself against the bully, letting the rage build until my hue was a flickering red.

"That supposed to impress me?" he snorted. "So what will it be, the easy way or the hard way?"

"I have another idea, how about you just back off," I said, letting the rage build. Because of what had happened with Anna-Beth I was reluctant to go this route, but I thought I could control it. I kept the rage tightly focused on this fellow and let it grow.

He laughed, I attacked. By habit I launched myself at

his mid-section hoping to take him down. I just sailed right through him.

He grinned, and said, "I love the hard way!" We circled each other until the house and Jesus was behind me. I had no idea what I was doing, I was just buying time. At that point he must have figured out that I was clueless, and his grin widened.

He spread his arms out to his side, and giving a grunt, swept them towards me. I felt something hit me and carry me back across the front yard, through the steps and into the crawl space under my house. Jesus was there too, so he must have been caught by this, whatever it was. Our forms had gone wispy and I felt weak.

We could hear him chuckling from the street, "I love the hard way!"

This just made me madder, and I had an idea. I moved through the floor up into the kitchen. I modulated my two fingers properly and stuck them in the GFI outlet. The current coursed through me for a few seconds before the breaker tripped adding sparks to my red hue.

Jesus stood there agape. I had told him about this, but he hadn't seen it before.

Lit up with the energy, I flew out the front door, spotted the bully, and bore down on him. I focused on modulating my density (maybe frequency is a better word) to match his. As I got closer I saw fear creep into his eyes.

I flew through him and turned back around. He stood there shaking, waving his arms, trying to throw the sparks off of him. It was my time to grin. "I like the hard way too!" I yelled, letting the energy turn my voice manic.

As I moved toward him he tensed his face, and with a "pop" he was gone.

JJTTSABD #4: *Bullies. Can't even get away from them in death.*

Interview Transcript
Janet Lynch / Nate Luca: Part 7

Janet: He's fighting ghosts now? Why is he fighting ghosts?

Tamara: I don't know; this is what he wrote.

Janet: Ghosts?

Nate: He couldn't stand bullies. If there are ghost bullies you know JJ would fight them.

Janet: I guess. (pause) I feel so bad that he found the house empty. I couldn't stay you know, I just couldn't stay. With JJ and his father gone, and Jean off to college it was just too much.

Nate: I know Ma, it's all right.

Transmission #35
Received 2010/12/08 03:45:21

I stood there for a time, the energy still sparking off of me, trying to figure out what to do next. I was literally amped up and had the equivalent of a big load of adrenaline running through me.

I paced the street as Jesus watched silently from a distance, but that didn't help. I had to dump this energy without hurting someone. I didn't want to hurt someone again.

Jesus called, "Get in the ground."

"Huh?"

"Just get in the ground, now!"

Having nothing better to do, I walked to the yard, and allowed myself to sink up to my neck. Soon, surprisingly, I began to feel more normal.

"How did you know?" I asked Jesus.

"That was electricity right? You run a wire from the lightning rod into the ground to 'ground' it."

I was impressed. About ten minutes like that and I was back to normal.

"Who was that?" Jesus asked.

"I have no idea, but I bet this Spencer guy is a lot worse."

"Sounds like it. We better get down to the courthouse."

"Yeah because I bet he's coming back, and he's gonna bring friends."

All thoughts of practicing form or a leisurely day went out the window. We flew at our best pace down to the courthouse and went into Ma's office.

Her desk was in a group of cubes with a few other recorders. Her desk was empty, all of her stuff gone. Jesus took the lead, looking for clues as to where she had gone.

"Being dead makes this hard," he said, "usually I would just ask someone." He paused looking around, "Is there a break room around here?"

"Sure, right over here." We went in and scoured the place.

"Over here JJ," he called.

I went over and on the bulletin board was a picture of Ma surrounded by coworkers, behind her was a banner, "You Can't Fire Me, I Retire!" She was smiling in the picture, but her face was strained and heavy; it was clearly a put on smile, not a genuine one.

"Wow, she retired," I said.

"That explains why she left town. Any idea where she would go?" Jesus asked.

"I don't know."

"She's been through a lot, where would she feel safest?"

"I would think here." She had spent that last three decades in Globe.

"Think, JJ, she just lost a son."

It seems impossible, but I had kinda forgotten that again. I mean, I felt alive, I was here in her office. Jesus's words brought it all rushing back to me and I felt the heaviness of depression coming on. "My sister. She would want to be closer to her other child."

"And where is she?"

"In Tucson, she goes to UA."

"Let's go."

I was still shaken and followed Jesus out of the building. Once we got outside, our bully was standing there, only this time he wasn't alone. He was flanked by two other poorly formed extra-corporeals. All three of them were missing their left pinkies, which was real odd, but I didn't have time to think about it. I knew there were probably more of them out of sight, covering the other exits.

The bully grinned. "I guess we are down to the harder way boys."

Jesus turned and looked at me. This had jolted me back to the present, but I wasn't in the mood for a fight I couldn't win. "It's time to fly. You with me man?"

I nodded.

Jesus leaped into the air, I followed him straight up. He looked back, cursed under his breath, and said, "Stay close."

I looked down and saw what he was cursing about. There was a group of eight ECs following us about fifty yards back and gaining. They must have been surprised by our flight and taken a moment to get it together.

It soon became clear what Jesus's plan was. He was heading into a group of small white cumulus clouds floating in the blue sky almost directly above us. It was a near thing; our bully was only a few yards behind me when we hit the cloud.

Jesus reached out his hand, which was well formed and solid, and said, "Take my hand, we can't get split up." I formed my hand the same way and clasped his. It felt solid and reassuring. Even as the cloud got dense we didn't lose each other.

He led us in a series of maneuvers—straight up to the outside edge of this cloud, skimming the edge of it, and flying quickly to a nearby, smaller cloud. Through that one and hopping to yet a smaller cloud where we stopped, floating horizontally right at the bottom of the cloud.

Globe lay below us, the Pinal Mountains to the south, and the pits, slag pile, and leach ponds of the Miami mining operations to the west.

"Keep your hand entwined with mine, but get as transparent as you can," Jesus whispered.

"Shouldn't we keep moving?"

"No, our movement will catch their attention. We should be OK; they are not very good at this. They should have left someone below the clouds to watch for us."

So we floated there as I let my form go wispy and transparent, willing it to be thin and insubstantial. At first this was hard, we had been spending so much time doing the opposite, but then it became easier. I felt a lightness that was appealing, so I went with that.

We could see our pursuers occasionally as they flew briefly out of one cloud into another, in an unorganized pattern, their grouping become less dense as they spread out. Eventually two of them headed for our cloud.

I became lighter and lighter, till my entwinement with Jesus's form faded and was barely noticeable. My vision suddenly shifted, and I could see everywhere at once: above, below, and around. A lethargy stole over me as I floated along, watching our pursuers with detached disinterest.

Two of them entered the cloud, entered me. At this point

my form was as large and diffuse as the cloud. They flew in and out and around. I could feel Jesus slowly shifting his position to get out of the way, but I didn't care. They couldn't hurt me, how could you hurt a cloud?

Minutes passed, then an hour. The rest of the clouds were mere wisps, the only one left was the me-cloud floating above the ground, the wind pushing me gently to the east. I watched my shadow as it caressed the ground below; I reveled in the warmth of the sun.

"Spencer's gonna be pissed," the bully said, he and the seven others were gathered below me. "They must have popped out—better go tell him the bad news." They flew back down, heading towards an old abandoned mine north of town.

When they had been gone for some minutes, I heard Jesus say, "JJ, JJ!"

I heard his voice, but it was too much of a bother to answer. Floating, that was all I wanted to do.

"What did you do? Come on JJ, snap out of it, we can go now." He went on like that for a time, but I didn't care. Everything was perfect; there was no need to change any-thing. I felt my connection to Jesus strengthen and grow strong, and then I felt a tug as he pulled me to the west.

I could still see everywhere: I could see Jesus's form, crisp but transparent, pulling me; I could see the other clouds next to me, I could see the sun bright above me, and I could see the land rolling below me.

He tugged and tugged, pulling me away from the cloud. I watched as it slowly separated from me and continued moving to the east.

That wasn't right, I was the cloud, it couldn't separate from me. It wasn't right. I tried to move back towards it, but

Jesus held firm, and soon the cloud and I were completely separated. I was sad, what had happened to me? Wasn't I the cloud? Hadn't I always been a cloud—untroubled in the sky blessing the hot land with my shadow, absorbing the beautiful warmth of the sun?

"JJ, Banquo is here." I could see everywhere, but I could not see Banquo. "Banquo is here JJ. He has more to teach us, but first he must see your form, your human form."

Banquo had secrets, secrets that I needed. Human form, I had a human form.

Slowly Jesus's words affected me; slowly my form became smaller, denser; slowly it became human.

Soon, my vision was of limited scope; soon I could see hands, and legs; soon I was back.

Sorrow followed me back. I missed what I had been; I missed the simplicity. When I was fully back to myself I said, "Jesus, you are a liar. Banquo is not here."

"Sorry man, I had to bring you back."

"Thanks." I still felt strange, and exhausted. "I'm so tired."

"Me too. Just let yourself fade, you'll wake up rested, back in Tucson."

I hated fading; the uncertainty of it troubled me deeply, but I was in no shape to argue. As soon as he suggested it, I was fading.

Transmission #36
Received 2010/12/08 05:00:12

When I came to, I was floating near Jesus in the graveyard across from Banquo. The sun was up; it appeared to
be about 10 a.m.

"Ah, there you are," Banquo said. "Kind of you to join us."

Disoriented, but not out of practice, I snapped into a
crisp nearly solid form.

"Good. Good," Banquo said. "Jesus here tells me you
have some things to share with me."

"I do?" I answered looking to Jesus.

"It's time. Banquo needs to know what you have been
up to." I had shared everything with Jesus, but hadn't told
very much to Banquo. I didn't think he would approve.

I felt betrayed, and it must have shown. Banquo said,
"Jesus has made a convincing case that the two of you need
more advanced training because of your..." he paused, his
eyes narrowing, "...experiences. I need to hear about them
directly from you."

I wasn't sure what to do. I looked from Banquo to Jesus.
Jesus gave me an encouraging nod.

"OK," I said. We spent the next few hours with the tale. I told him everything, pretty much as presented here. He asked questions from time to time, particularly about the things I had discovered how to do and the ghosts we encountered in Globe.

After the story was over, Banquo was silent for a long time, much longer than I was comfortable with. When I couldn't take the silence any longer, I blurted out, "Please don't tell me I'm the 'chosen one' prophesied from long ago, come here to do great things."

As soon as I said it, I regretted it. I didn't believe it, but I was struggling to find an explanation. I had no idea if my experiences were normal or not; if everyone could do these strange things. My doubt, and fear, and nervousness mixed with too many works of heroic fiction created that utterly awkward statement.

Banquo said nothing for a long thirty seconds, his face serious, until he burst out with a rumbling belly laugh. The laugh stretched out while I felt myself grow hot with embarrassment, a pink hue flickering along the edges of my form.

"No my boy. No. If there are any such prophecies, I know nothing about them." His face grew serious, and kind. "But you are talented with how you use, and abuse, your form. That is not in doubt." That helped the sting fade a bit. "And I have to agree with Jesus," he continued, "you both need accelerated training. The path you are on requires it."

"Path? What path am I on?"

"Most spirits that are here, like us, have something left to do. Most take their time getting it done, but you dived right in."

I feared sounding dense, but asked, "What am I doing?"

"Finishing up your life. First you sought revenge for your

death, then you tried to clean up that mess, and now you are trying to make sure your loved ones are well."

He was right of course. I had been going on instinct, and hadn't put it together. "Of course."

"Here is what we are going to do," Banquo began, back in professor mode. "The two of you go about doing what you need to do, and I will find you every morning that I am available, and aid you if I can."

I opened my mouth to say something, but thought better of it after my last outburst. I wanted to say: *Is that all you got? Can't you just give us the lay of the land? Tell us what to expect?* But all I actually said was, "Thank you Banquo, that would be a great help."

Transmission #37
Received 2010/12/09 02:35:33

Eventually my coffee time with Tam became a bit more formal as our "out of the lab" friendship grew. At the end of one we would tentatively plan our next time together. It was just casual and friendly, but I really looked forward to it, and I like to think that she did too.

During our coffees, the mystery of John, her dead fiancé, and the origins of SECI slowly became clear.

Tam, if you are not comfortable with this information being known, then feel free to edit all of this out. You are my friend and it is your secret to share, not mine. Personally I think you are ready, I think you are strong enough.

The next thing I learned was the circumstances of his death, and it wasn't pretty.

One day she showed me a picture on her cell phone. It was a close-up of Tamara and a handsome man, their heads close together, big smiles on their faces. He had a round face, sandy hair, big brown eyes, and a crescent shaped scar on his cheek.

"That's John, he was murdered," she said.

"Murdered?"

She sighed and nodded her head yes.

"Do you... Do you want to talk about it?" I asked, adding, "You don't have to if you don't want to."

"No, no, I think I need to. You've been open about your dad and what you went through after he died so I know you understand."

"Yeah, I do." After someone really close to you dies, something changes in you. It's kind of like a club with a secret handshake. It is really hard to talk about that kind of experience with someone who hasn't been there. Deep grief is not something you can just talk or rationalize your way out of. Grieving is a process that has to run its course (all those damn stages), and the course it runs is not easy or pretty or predictable, and it can't be fit into some little box or remedied by some cute phrase or aphorism.

Hearing things like "he is in a better place now" drove me crazy after my dad died. It assumed that the bulk of my grieving experience was worrying about his immortal soul—it wasn't; I was coping with having someone I dearly loved ripped out of my life. And yes, it was largely a selfish and personal experience, but that is just the way of it.

The other thing that drove me nuts was when well-intentioned people, knowing I was suffering, asked me over and over how I was doing. It was like torture. When asked, I would say something nonspecific like "OK," or "fine," but what I really wanted to say was "Oh, for the first time in a few days I was experiencing a moment not soaked in grief, but now that you have asked me how I am you have reminded me how terrible things are and thrown me right back into it. Thanks, thanks a lot."

And really, is our society good at talking about death,

about living with the reality of mortality? Hell no. It's not surprising that we are so bad at dealing with it.

Having both been down that road, Tam and I spoke the same language, as it were. So I didn't push Tam, I was just open and listened.

"It was a mugging; he was stabbed to death." She paused then for a long, long time. I just sat there listening. I know, I know, she wasn't talking so you might be wondering what was I listening to? If you have to ask then I don't think I can really explain it, but I will try. I was listening to what she wasn't saying. I was hearing how hard this was for her to share, how much courage it was taking her to speak. I was listening and not talking because that is what she needed.

"I remember it like it was yesterday," she said when she finally continued. "We had just had dinner and we were going to see a movie. While I was paying the bill he left to get some cash from an ATM that was just around the corner. When I got there he was lying on the ground, blood pouring out of a hole in his chest, gasping for breath.

"I called 911 and held him while we waited for the ambulance to come. He looked at me with these wide, wide eyes; he must have been in tremendous pain, but there was something he wanted to say. His lips moved, but barely a sound escaped, so I leaned close.

"I didn't know it then, but a lung had been collapsed and was filling up with blood from the wound. He couldn't really talk but he tried, he tried so hard to tell me something, but only a few intelligible phrases came out: 'Tam, I...,' 'Must tell you where...,' 'I should have...,' 'Sorry.'

"He died that night on the operating table." After that she got up and left, we didn't talk about it again for some weeks.

Transmission #38
Received 2010/12/09 03:01:14

We stayed the night; we both needed the rest, and had a good time at the Midnight Circle.

Banquo recited for us, "Waiting for Godot." Behind him different Circle members cycled through pantomiming the actions of Vladimir, Estragon, and the other characters. It is an odd play, one that I had never seen or read before. Full of heavy apathy and depression as the two main characters wait for Godot, who never appears. They are caught in their waiting, unable to change.

I saw much of my own life in it—all the years I had shuffled along without real purpose or drive. It seemed to me that it was even easier to get lost in the waiting once you are dead. I wandered off alone and spent the rest of the night in a melancholy mood. I avoided the bardo only by experience and when the morning came I was restless.

"Can we go now?" I asked Jesus as soon as I found him.

He looked me over and with a grin said, "Can you get dressed first?"

I looked at myself with a start. I wasn't naked, but I

wasn't "dressed" as defined by Banquo. My form was a diffuse mess. I concentrated and brought my form into focus: jeans, shoes, and a long sleeve black t-shirt. It took a few minutes, and I felt better, more myself, when I was done.

We raced off to the U, working on our speed and landed in front of Jean's dorm. I took the lead and we "walked" in and up the stairs, continuing our form practice. We walked right through the door into her room. It was a two person setup with Jean's side empty—she must have moved out recently. "Really!" I shouted. Jesus chuckled and started looking around the room.

It wasn't long before he pointed at a white-board on the door, that said, "Jean's new digs: 2100 E. Roger Rd, #J12."

"You know where that is at?" Jesus asked.

"No idea."

We stayed there for a while discussing how to deal with this. If we were corporeal, it would be a simple matter, but since we were not, we had to either find a map, or stumble across it.

We deduced a few things: 1) It wouldn't be too close to the university, that would make it more expensive than she could afford; 2) It was not on a main street, otherwise I would have remembered the name. We decided to fly down the main roads in a grid pattern until we found Roger Road.

We headed out east on Speedway going fast at the level of the street signs. We turned north on Country Club, west on Grant, south on Oracle, and spiraled out from there.

It was slow at first; we had to make sure we saw every sign. We eventually found a rhythm. I would go out front, and slow down right when I got to the street sign while Jesus zoomed past. He would then slow down for the next sign as I flew past. We went back and forth like that and got our rate up to about thirty miles per hour.

It only took a couple hours until we found it. Rogers Road is a few miles north of campus and intersects with Oracle. From there we followed it east until we found the apartments. They are just south of the Rillito River and just north of Tucson General Hospital. They call it a river, but it is just a wash—in the southwest you take what you can get. It only runs when a monsoon hits.

The apartment complex was pretty large with several hundred units. The buildings were brown two-story numbers probably about twenty or thirty years old. There was a swimming pool and lots of palm trees. And that's where we found Ma, in the swimming pool. We were searching for building J, but came across the pool first, and there she was.

She had a big hat on, and was floating in the water as easy as could be. I don't know what I expected, but this wasn't it. I felt relieved, but then I felt disappointed. Hadn't my death had more of an effect than that?

"I'm going to leave you with this JJ," Jesus said. "I'll be up there if you need me." He pointed to the roof of one of the apartment buildings, which he promptly flew to.

The world doesn't stop. There was Ma, living her life, taking an afternoon dip. The world doesn't stop.

I got closer, immersed myself in the water too, and I could hear her hum. It was strangely familiar, but it took a while for me to recognize it. I went with that, letting the irritation of not knowing what song she was humming take over. It was better, safer than dealing with what I was feeling.

After a while she sung, real soft, "Chain... chain..." her words faltering as she tried to continue. That did it; I recognized it as a Fleetwood Mac song, a band my mother is very fond of.

The recognition broke the spell, and I really looked at her. She wasn't "OK." I could see it in her face. Floating in a pool by herself, this wasn't like her. Retiring and moving to Tucson to live with my sister (as I would soon confirm) wasn't like her. I felt terrible, so terrible about being disappointed. She wasn't OK, and I wished she was. But that, as I well know, is not the way of grief. There are all these stages to go through, and Ma was on her own personal journey through it.

Transmission #39
Received 2010/12/10 04:45:16

Jesus is a wise man (sorry, I can't help myself with stuff like that—the name just makes it too easy). He accompanied me for the next few days as I watched over my mother, but he kept his distance. We spent nights at the graveyard; I needed the comfort of the Midnight Circle. Every day around dawn we would fly up to those apartments. Jesus spent the day on the roof, and I spent the day watching her, following her. After she went to bed, we would fly back to the graveyard.

Jean was gone most of the day, off at school, but she spent nights with Ma, and they often talked of me, and Ma often cried.

It was difficult, but I had little choice. This was the hard work of Stage #5: Acceptance.

I had to accept that I was gone, and that I couldn't do anything about it. I had to accept that my mother was hurt and grieving, and I couldn't do anything about it. I had to accept that soon I would fade into the background as she got on with her life, and that is the way it should be.

I contemplated trying to communicate with her like I did Anna-Beth, but I couldn't. I couldn't risk scaring her, or something going wrong. I couldn't risk turning her from her path. She had gotten through my father's death; I knew she could get through mine.

When it became too much, or I needed to give her privacy, I would fly up to the roof and sit with Jesus. We often didn't say much; we just sat there looking out over the city laid out before us.

I hope that I can be that good of a friend to him someday. When I was silent, he would just sit there with me, when I needed to distract myself with conversation he was there for that too. He never asked me how I was doing, or if I was all right (I clearly wasn't, and those questions just make that obvious).

Jesus knew grief, that much was clear, and he didn't seem as afraid of it as most people are. He allowed me my grief, which is a hard thing to do.

I used to think that the dying had the easier part of the bargain: they were done, off to a better place. Now I know it is not always that simple.

Our second morning there, we were up on the roof when Banquo popped in. He wanted to know what was going on, so I told him. He was silent for a while, an appraising look on his face, before he said, "Remember after Anna-Beth was injured, and you held her head?"

I nodded my head yes.

"That detached, but loving state?"

I nodded my head again.

"That is the best thing you can do for your mother. When you are near her, feel that warmth flowing from you into her. It helps to be touching her, but you don't have to."

He stayed for a while with us up on the roof. He had me practice on Jesus, and Jesus practiced on me. It was a tricky state to get into, but by the time he left we had both done it, and "felt" it.

So that is what I did every day. I tried to feel the love and let the warmth flow from me to her in the gentlest way possible. She would often lie down for a nap in the afternoon, and I would put my hands on her head like I had with Anna-Beth.

I wasn't always successful with it, but I got better at it. And when it did work, it was wonderful. I got to be with Ma, know I was dead, know she was grieving, and still be OK. Precious moments, although often brief, of acceptance.

On about my fifth day of doing this she went down for a long nap, and it really worked. I felt the warmth flowing easily; I felt detached from what would happen; I felt like I was really there with her, that there was no separation.

That night when Jean came home she said, "I took a nap today and the strangest thing happened."

"What Ma?"

"Well I had a splitting headache when I laid down, but felt great when I got up. That's not strange. The strange part is the dream I had."

"Dream?" Jean asked.

"Yes, a dream. I dreamed about JJ." She paused, her eyes tearing up.

Jean stopped and sat down across from her, "Go on."

"He was sitting on a roof next to a Mexican man with a big mustache. They were talking. JJ said, 'I just wish she knew I was OK.'" She paused.

"Was that it Ma?"

"Pretty much. It was real short, but it felt like him, it felt like JJ." Tears were falling down her checks now. Jean took her hand. "Do you think it was him, do you think it was JJ?"

Jean surprised me then. Tears were forming in her eyes as she said, "I do Ma, I do."

"And you know," Ma added, "that roof looked like this roof."

Interview Transcript
Janet Lynch / Nate Luca: Part 8

Janet: Oh my God!

Tamara: What?

Janet: My dream was real. I saw JJ and that Jesus man. The dream was real!

Tamara: So you can confirm the accuracy of the conversation?

Janet: Yes! Yes! (crying) My boy, my boy is really OK, isn't he?

Tamara: (crying) Yes, he is.

Janet: (embracing Luca): This is real Nate, this is real! Nate: I know. I know.

Transmission #40
Received 2010/12/11 01:58:19

One of those days up on the roof when I needed a break I asked Jesus something that I had wanted to ask for a long time. "So," I began, "how do you reconcile 'this,'" I pointed to the two of us, indicating our ghostly nature, "with your faith."

He thought for a moment and said, "If I truly have faith, I have no need to reconcile 'this.'"

He had me there; I chewed on that for a while, letting the silence deepen around us. "Hmmm," I finally said, "you don't strike me as the blind faith type."

Jesus chuckled, "But isn't faith, to a certain degree, blind?"

"You know what I mean."

"I do," Jesus agreed.

"So?"

He chuckled again. "If you are looking for an authoritative answer on Christianity and our current experience I don't have it."

"Now you are just avoiding the question!"

"OK, OK. Reconciling it is not hard. Perhaps this is heaven and we are being tested, kind of an entrance exam."

I snorted. "Ha! Now you *are* making things up—you never struck me as the over rationalizing, 'I'm always right,' kind."

Jesus held his hands up. "I surrender, señor." We lapsed into silence and I gave him time to think. "The truth my friend, you want the truth?" he finally asked.

"Please," I answered.

"I don't know."

"Wow, that makes two of us," I said. "I was raised going to church, but never really thought much about it all. I don't recall anything in the Bible about ghosts."

"Me neither. The only spirits it talks about are angels and demons. After death is judgment and then heaven or hell. If you are not quite ready for heaven then it's off to the cleansing fire of purgatory."

"Purgatory. Hmmm, think we are in purgatory?" I asked.

Jesus shrugged his shoulders and said, "I don't know, and frankly I don't need to know: I have faith."

"Faith?" He wasn't making sense now. "Faith in what?"

"Faith in God. Faith in there being a purpose for our experiences, even this one."

"Even though it doesn't make sense?"

"Especially because it doesn't make sense. By definition God is much, much smarter than me—I don't expect to understand his ways."

I was getting irritated, "So you believe all this will magically work itself out because God knows best?"

"God knows everything."

"Oh come on!"

Jesus smiled, "Standard evangelical doctrine holds

that Jesus died for our sins and accepting him as savior is all that is needed. But Mother Dominga taught me that meritorious works contribute to salvation and also help to atone for past sins."

"So," I said, thinking about his statement, "you're more along the lines of, 'God helps those who help themselves'?"

"Yes. I am not waiting for any magic or a 'get out of hell free' card. I continue to be the best and do the best I can. The big questions I don't worry about. I just worry about doing the best I can each day."

We talked more about faith and religion that day; about sin, redemption, and the afterlife. Jesus's faith in God was solid, but not his faith in man. He wasn't inclined to a 100% literal interpretation of the Bible. "Man has been in there too many times," he said, "writing it, editing, deciding which scriptures would be in it, translating it from its native language. I believe in the perfection of God, not the perfection of the Bible. The Bible is not what I worship. If you study how the Bible was put together it was a very long and decidedly human process."

I finished our conversation stunned. That strong sense of right and wrong, that steady compass Jesus had, so reminded me of Nate. It came from a more religious direction, but it was the same thing. The thought briefly flashed in my mind, but was quickly chased out; I was not ready to go there yet.

Transmission #41
Received 2010/12/11 02:45:16

"She felt you JJ, she felt you and Jesus," Banquo said the next day when I told him about my mother's dream. We were on the roof of Ma's apartment.

"How?"

"I think her sleeping put her in a receptive state, which, coupled with your work, got through to her."

"Can I do it again? Can I get a message of my choosing to her?"

"I don't know JJ. The deeper you both are, the better the chances. But, you already did get a message to her, and an important one. What else do you need to say?"

I paused for a while, and realized that I mostly just wanted to communicate with her again—in any way. "Umm, I want to tell her I love her."

"OK. Then you know what to do."

Ma and I fell into a ritual. She would lie down every afternoon at about 2 p.m. She would carefully prepare the space before lying down: getting the pillows just right; drawing the shades; turning the ringer off on the phone.

She wanted another dream and I wanted her to have one. I would be there every day with her doing my best to feel the warmth and the love flow into her. It didn't work well for a few days. Either she was restless, or I couldn't get into the state I needed to be in. I think we both wanted it too much.

On the fifth day I felt it click and sunk into it. I gently added a message, letting it flow with the energy to her.

After we were done I waited expectantly for Sis to come home; I wanted to hear Ma tell her about it. I was restless and went up to the roof with Jesus and watched for her car.

When she finally got home, I rushed down eager to hear what Ma had to say.

"I had a dream," she announced as Jean came in, but her tone was somber.

"JJ?" Jean asked.

"No, Nate."

Nate? Nate! I was swept up in this sense of guilt. I had been avoiding the thought of him. Not consciously, but when Ma mentioned him it was clear that I had been in denial about Nate; about finishing with Nate.

"What did you dream?"

"He was in the ocean, up to his neck. The waves kept crashing on him, tossing him about. I tried to reach him, but the water kept dragging me back to shore. I called his name, but he couldn't hear me."

"How is Nate doing?" Jean asked. "Do you know?"

"I don't. I have been so busy... No! That's not it. I just haven't been able to face him since the funeral."

Jean went to her and said something, but I didn't hear it. I headed up and out of the building to the roof.

Jesus looked at me and said, "What's wrong?"

"Nate. I forgot about Nate."

Transmission #42
Received 2010/12/11 03:20:12

JJTTSABD #5: *Even when you are dead, you don't escape the toughest parts about being alive.*

Guilt sucks, it truly does. It sucks the life right out of you, and that is what happened to me on that roof with Jesus. The denial I had built up around me was slowly being stripped away, each layer a painful challenge, each a difficult step.

A wail escaped my chest giving voice to my guilt, to my grief, and I sunk quickly into bardo-land. Jesus tried valiantly to keep me from sliding down, but this time there was just no stopping me.

I was closer to Nate than I was to any other human being; the pain of knowing what this had done to him combined with my own pain was overwhelming. It took me straight to the bardo.

I was on that beach Ma had described, and Nate was struggling to keep his head above water. He saw me and cried out "JJ! Help!" I ran in trying to reach him, but the waves threw me back on shore leaving me exhausted.

I would lie there panting, listening to his pleas, watching him go under again and again, until a shred of energy came back to me. I would then thrust myself back into the water, only to be tossed onto the shore by the waves.

I cried out to him, but he didn't seem to hear me. He just kept calling "JJ, help! JJ, where are you?"

After a very long time, a bent and wizened man came walking down the beach towards me. His skin was white with deep wrinkles, his hair grey, his left arm missing.

"Help! Help us," I cried. "My friend, can you help my friend?"

He paused and looked me over. "Why yes, I could if I had two good arms. Give me yours and I will get him out."

"I... My arm?"

"Yes boy, your left arm."

"I don't know how."

"Well, can I have it?"

"I guess so."

The man then reached over and popped off my left arm as if I was some cheap action figure, and put it onto himself. It didn't hurt at all. He flexed my hand (now his hand), and said, "Good." He marched into to the water, the waves giving him no problems, and he dragged Nate out.

Nate lay panting on the beach, looked up at the man and said, "Thank you sir."

"Nate! Nate! I'm here," I cried as I ran over to him. He couldn't hear me or see me.

The man, with my arm, promptly walked down the beach.

While Nate lay there panting I kept trying to get his attention, but couldn't. I tried to touch him, but my hand went right through him. I tried and tried until I was exhausted again and just laid on the beach next to him.

When I had been silent for a while, Nate raised his head up as if he had heard something, and looked out to the ocean and said, "JJ? JJ? I'm coming JJ."

He was soon back in the water getting pummeled by the waves unable to leave, calling for my help. I tried to go in and help him, but with only one arm I did worse than before.

After another long period of this, the man came back down the beach. He still had my left arm, I recognized it, but was now missing his right arm. We went through the whole cycle again. He took my right arm, rescued Nate only to have Nate go back in when he thought he heard me calling.

With no arms I was even less successful until eventually the wizened old man came down the beach again. This time he was missing his left leg and slowly hopping on his right. After I gave him my leg, he got Nate out, but soon Nate went back in looking for me.

Once more we did this, and I gave him my right leg, with the same results. Nate ended up back in the water stuck, and I lay helpless on the beach without any arms or legs.

I can't tell you how long this went on, but it felt like forever. Finally I gave up, I gave into my helplessness. I just lied there on my back, listening to the waves, listening to Nate's cries, staring at the sun.

The sun was a big yellow ball above me in a hazy sky: hot, placid, eternal. The sun didn't care about our struggles; the sun wasn't moved by our pain; it just stayed the same.

As I focused on the sun, I started to feel just a little bit calmer, so I focused on it more. It wasn't a straight path, but soon the sun became bigger, and brighter, until it dominated my field of vision. It became hotter and closer until I could hear it pop and crackle.

It came closer and closer, the heat becoming more and more intense, until I realized the sizzling sound wasn't the sun, it was me. I didn't care though: I wanted to be like the sun, let it consume me, let me become it.

The yellow orb was soon all I could see, and the sizzling got so loud that it was all I could hear.

And then there was no more sun, no more sizzling, no more me.

Transmission #43
Received 2010/12/12 02:16:21

If you have any kind of life (or speaking from personal experience, any kind of death), things get weird. Tamara's fiancé John's death was weird.

He was apparently mugged and stabbed to death in a good neighborhood near the university, and he used his last moments with his beloved attempting to communicate something important and cryptic to her. It took a while, but she finally did bring it back up during coffee time.

"I bet you are wondering about John," she said.

"Ahh... Yeah," I answered, taking a sip of my coffee. "Actually it's driving me nuts."

She smiled and said, "It is kind of you not to push."

"You'll tell me when you are ready. It does no good to force these kinds of things." Silence descended, but since she had brought it up, I asked her, "So is this why you did SECI? You wanted to talk to him, ask him what he was trying to say?"

She sighed. "Yes. But it gets pretty complicated."

"Doesn't it always?"

She smiled thinly and nodded. "I thought I knew John, knew him better than anyone else in my life. But..." She stared down into her cappuccino, a faraway look in her eyes. "You find out things about someone after they die. When my grandmother died my mom found this huge cache of food in the garage. Unbelievable really, canned goods at least fifty years old. She had been hording food for decades and none of us ever knew about it.

"When John died I found out some surprising things about him. He was studying engineering at the university just like Jin and I, but was a couple years ahead of us; actually that is how we met, at school. He was working for one of the professors doing some kind of top secret research; he could never talk about it.

"We had been living together, and after he died, the FBI came and took everything. Computers, books, paperwork; everything really except for clothes and dishes. I was reeling, still in shock from the trauma of his death and now this. The next day they came and took me in for questioning. They grilled me for hours about our relationship, about his work and what I knew about it, about what he had said when he died. They had pictures of us together that were over a year old. They had been watching us."

She stopped speaking, her eyes wide from the remembered fear. "That must have been terrible," I said.

She nodded. "The worst part..." she choked out. "The worst part is that they believed he was murdered, and may have been leaking classified military intelligence."

That spooked me. I looked around the café; I am not sure what I expected, but somehow I thought she must be under surveillance or something, even though it had been two years since he died. "Who do they think killed him?"

"They didn't tell me much, but they suspected that he had stopped leaking information about the project and was killed because of it. That professor he worked for was never seen again after the night John was killed."

I was stunned; I mean, what do you say? There is weird, and there is *weird*. And that was *weird*. It's the kind of thing you see on TV all the time, but never expect to encounter in the real world.

Transmission #44
Received 2010/12/12 03:01:15

The sun was my escape from the bardo. It might seem obvious that what you need to do is focus on something besides your pain to get out, but it is far from easy. It is asking yourself to be conscious when you are unconscious. It is like becoming lucid enough in a bad dream to realize you are dreaming and wake yourself up, except harder, much harder. I never knew I was in the bardo, I just finally gave up, and finding relief in focusing on the sun, I found my way out. I was lucky.

I came to with a fright. A semi was barreling down on me. I cringed and covered myself, but it just passed right through me. After a few more cars had run through me I came to my senses, and flew up out of the way.

I was just above the interstate. It didn't take me long to figure out it was I-10, and with a little flying I found that I was just outside of Tucson on the way to Nate's place.

My next step seemed obvious: I flew to Nate's house.

Nate lived on a small island of private property surrounded by BLM land off of I-10 between Tucson and Picacho Peak.

You had to take a little dirt road, off of a highway frontage road, a couple miles back into the desert. He lived in a single wide trailer.

When I got there, his tow truck was gone; he must have been out on a call. He inherited this place, and the business, from his uncle, who he lived with after college. His uncle had cancer, and didn't get along well enough with his own children for any of them to help him. He wanted to stay home, so big Nate stepped up.

He handled it like he did everything else. It was the right thing to do, so he just did it. His uncle showed him the business, and Nate took care of him. At first it wasn't much, but as the disease took its course, it became more and more and more.

Uncle Sal (which is what I called him too), was an eccentric old fart. He collected coins, was obsessed with watching (not playing) golf, and would only drink Corona in a bottle with a half lime squeezed into it.

The process for the Corona preparation was very exacting. The beer had to be from a bottle, and be ice cold. You had to open it, pour off an ounce or so into another glass, take the lime (always fresh), cut it in half, and using a funnel squeeze all of the lime juice into the bottle. You then put the bottle in a cozy and delivered both the bottle and the glass with the extra beer in it. He would knock back the extra beer, and slowly nurse the limed bottle.

He wasn't a bad eccentric; he was just one of those guys you couldn't spend less than three hours with. You would drop by on your way out of town to say hello, and he would start on one of his stories, like a ninety-minute dissertation on the metal makeup of the penny over the years.

And he truly loved pennies. One sure way to piss him

off was to suggest that we no longer had a need for such a small denomination. You might as well have declared World War III. He would spit and huff, and not stop arguing with you, even if it took days, until you had come around to his point of view. And if you suggested we didn't need physical currency at all he would probably grab his shotgun and chase you off of his property.

I saw him do it once. He chased someone off his property with a shotgun. Nate and I were pulling in for a visit when a man in a suit came tearing out of the trailer with Sal hot on his heels. The man sprinted to his car and tore off with Sal shooting in the car's general direction.

He must have seen my look of disbelief because when he walked by me he said, "What!? It was just buckshot; I couldn't have really hurt him."

Uncle Sal was also a Civil War buff, more specifically, he was an expert on "the westernmost conflict of the Civil War." It took place just down I-10 at Picacho Peak in 1862. I think that may have been why he settled himself out here. He was one of those guys who dressed up, rode horses, and participated in the reenactment every March.

When he got sick, he didn't get his limed Corona for a long time, and it made him cross. When he was really sick, when the final outcome became clear, he had as many as he wanted. Nate knew the end was near when he stopped asking for them at all.

Colon cancer is what got Uncle Sal, and I saw enough, and heard even more from Nate, to know that is not the way I wanted to die. As it turns out, I got to go quick. From this side, I don't really know if there is a "good" way to go. Gone is gone.

Uncle Sal was so grateful to Nate, and so pissed at his kids, that he left everything to Nate.

After college I lived here for about a year with Nate, when going through my post-Dad, post-Rhiannon meltdown, and I spent a lot of time there even after that.

In high school Nate and I took auto shop together, which was mostly a joke for me. I had known all the basics for years, but what I did discover is that Nate was great at figuring out what was wrong with a car (that process of elimination that I was never good at), but was terrible at the doing—his big hands hampered him, and he often over-played his strength. We made a great team, he was good at figuring out what to do, and I was good at doing it.

After my dad died I swore off the whole mechanic thing. The sights and smells just reminded me of him too much. But with Nate's and my therapist's prodding I slowly got back into it. I helped Nate keep the tow truck in shape, and then we started fixing up and reselling old cars. Nate knew all the local garages, and would come across the deals. He was great with assessing the value of the car, and estimating what we could sell it for, and what it would take to fix it. I would come out most weekends and we would work on cars and, in a salute to Uncle Sal, drink limed Coronas.

It was hard at first; I couldn't deny my father's death when I was working on cars. But, in the long run it was healing. Once I got so I really enjoyed doing it again, I came into a better place with my dad. I started to be able to remember the good times, what I loved about him again, not just the bad times and the pain.

So, when I got there, the tow truck was gone, but our latest project was not: a 1992 Mustang GT convertible. It sat there tarped, just like it had been the last time I worked on it. Next to it was the junker Mustang that Nate had hauled over from the junk yard; we were using it for parts.

These older cars were popular with rich guys in their late fifties or early sixties. It took them back to the "good old days."

I felt happy to see the car, but sad too. Nate and I were a team, what was he going to do now? What was I going to do now?

I went into the trailer and looked around. The living room was a mess. Beer cans (cans! Uncle Sal would have had a fit) and empty tequila bottles everywhere, along with half eaten food. The "guest" bedroom, where I was the guest 90% of the time, was just as I had left it. The door was closed, and nothing had been touched. The kitchen had dishes piled everywhere and Nate's room had mounds of dirty clothes lying about. Now neither Nate nor I were all that neat (except with tools), but we were not at this level.

I couldn't take it; I flew up and sat on the roof. Now that I was here, I had no idea what I was going to do. Ma, as hard as it was, was moving on. Nate obviously was not. Could I help him? I had to try.

I felt worried, guilty (a twisted version of "survivor's guilt"), and very, very unsure of myself.

Transmission #45
Received 2010/12/12 04:32:17

I've been thinking about personal entropy lately; the way life can sweep you along and take you down a path you never conceived of or ever really chose. After college it was like that for Nate and me.

Nate got swept up in caring for his Uncle Sal, and then taking over the business. I got lost in losing my dad and Rhiannon. I never intended to make a career of being a janitor; it was just a part-time college gig to help pay the bills. After what I had gone through, though, I couldn't muster the energy to change my direction and just fell into it full-time.

I didn't realize it yet, sitting there on Nate's roof, but death was turning into the same thing: I was getting swept up.

In many ways I don't think I really grew up while I was alive. Getting through high school, going to college—you don't choose that. That is just floating down the river, going where society wants you to go. I think for many there is a moment after you are done with school that you figure out what you really want. I missed that. So, I had been swept along by this process of dying until I had been deposited here on Nate's roof. I didn't think it out, I didn't plan it, I just reacted my way here.

I sat there for two hours before Nate got home, and thought, really thought; maybe for the first time in a long time. Why was I here? What was I trying to accomplish? Where did I want to go with my life (err... death)?

After what I had seen of Nate at my funeral my next step was clear: help him. I couldn't move on, I couldn't "graduate" until I knew he was OK. But, sitting there alone on his roof I took it a step further. After I helped Nate what then? Banquo's Lesson #5 stated that, "This is not the End," but what is next? Could I stick around here for a while and if so what would I do?

These thoughts were pinging around my head when I heard a pop, and Banquo was standing beside me.

"There you are," he said, his look appraising. Without hardly thinking about it I tightened up my form, which wasn't bad to start with. "What happened?" he asked. I gave him a brief synopsis of my time in bardo-land.

"Got yourself out of the Bardo this time, now that's progress!" he boomed. "Jesus saw you go down, and tried to help. By the time I showed up he had lost you. It's taken me a while to find you."

"Yeah, I think I faded for a while after getting out."

"That would explain it."

We were silent for a few minutes, staring at the string of lights moving down I-10 in the distance, when one of those lights broke off from the road and started heading this way.

That snapped me out of my reverie, "Listen Banquo, I think my next step is to help Nate," I said pointing to the two headlights slowly making their way towards us.

"Very well. Let's wait for him and see how he is doing."

"Why don't you take a look down there," I said pointing down to the trailer. "How he is doing is pretty clear."

Banquo sunk into the trailer and was back shortly, his face grim. "Not normal, I take it," he asked.

"No. Definitely not."

"Look at me JJ." I took my eyes off of the lights now getting close, the rumble of the truck discernable, and looked at Banquo. "As long as you think this is your fault, you won't be able to help."

I turned away, looking back at the truck. How do you respond to that? Oh yeah, it's not my fault, might as well go have a party! I chewed on that briefly and replied, "I need to help him for *me*." Some of that therapy crap had stuck I guess.

"Very well then, you must find a way to reach him."

"How?"

"There is no standard answer to that query my boy; everyone grieves in their own way. It could just take time."

I bit back a biting retort and instead said, "Any guesses?"

"You know him JJ, he's your best friend; what do you think will work?"

I honestly didn't know, but I thought about what would work for me. Nate and I were alike enough that it would be a good starting point. For myself, something physical would be necessary, something undeniable. A dream might have worked for my mom, but it wouldn't have worked for me and probably wouldn't work for Nate.

"Thanks," I said to Banquo, "that helps."

"Jesus has been worried about you; do you want me to bring him out?"

I thought for a moment and said, "No thanks. Tell him I appreciate the offer but I need to do this one alone."

Just then Nate pulled the tow truck up, got out, and headed for the trailer. He looked bad: a wrinkled, probably slept in, t-shirt, dirty hair, and an unshaved face.

"Very well," Banquo said, and *pop* he was gone.

Transmission #46
Received 2010/12/13 01:16:45

Nate's days were simple and repetitive. He would get up at about 1 p.m., call into dispatch and start his on-call time. While he waited, and in between calls, he would play games or watch sports. After his last tow he would get some take-out, come home, watch more sports and drink until he passed out.

Not that unusual, except for the passing out part. It wasn't like he was sitting around crying or anything, but he wasn't doing a thing beyond what he had to. He walked around with his jaw set, and his face tight; as if he could just keep putting one foot in front of the other he would eventually be OK.

His phone would ring, but he would only pick up for dispatch, and he never checked his messages. He did manage to shower a couple of times a week, and then would sift through the piles of clothes in his bedroom looking for the least dirty to put on.

His demeanor with his clients was not aggressive, but they often got scared. He was this big hulk of a man, who looked terrible, and barely spoke.

I spent twenty-four hours with him before I tried anything. I just went where he did (except for the bathroom, you've got to give a guy some privacy) observing him and thinking.

No, a dream wouldn't do it for me and probably wouldn't work for Nate. I wasn't sure that turning things off and on would work either. It had to be something undeniable, something tangible, something clearly visible. I had created visible light briefly during my haunting of William and Anna-Beth, but I hadn't had much practice, and I wasn't sure I could do it again. My second night with him I gave it a shot.

There was a pretty big mirror behind the couch (an attempt to make the cramped space look bigger I expect), and I put myself in front of Nate and started modulating my EM emissions down into the light spectrum.

It was slow tough work, but that first night I did produce few brief flashes, but Nate didn't seem to notice. The flat-screen was throwing off a lot more light than I was.

I wasn't disappointed though, I just kept at it. Each night for about the next week while he watched TV I worked on radiating in the visible spectrum. It was slow going, but I got better. I could create a small ball of light about the size of an orange, and sustain it pretty well. That night I think Nate did notice it because he kept looking funny at the screen as if there was something wrong with it. He thought what I was doing was his flat-screen malfunctioning.

It was clear I needed to turn it off, and I knew how to do that, but not when I was in "visible light" mode. I spent the next two nights figuring out how to emanate light with one part of my form, and modulate myself for electrical work with another.

And it worked, finally. My light was smaller, about the size of a ping-pong ball, but I was able to maintain it, and switch the screen off too.

"What the!" Nate said as he poked the remote turning the screen back on. I turned it back off, he turned it back on. He did this for several minutes until he gave up and finally noticed the light.

"Hey, what is that?" he slurred, pointing at me. Well I had gotten his attention, now what? I started moving the light in a small circle growing it in size. His eyes followed the light.

"Wow!" he said, looking at the can in his hand, "I guess I've had enough for tonight." He stumbled into the bedroom and promptly passed out. I tried turning the light on to get his attention again, but he was too far gone.

I spent the next day thinking about what my next move should be. I definitely needed to get the flat-screen off ASAP, before he was drunk, but what then? How could I communicate with him? I came up with a scheme: move the light up and down for yes; side to side for no; and circle with the light for something I can't answer.

After we did the TV on and off dance and Nate had given up, I spun the light in a tight circle in front of him.

"What the hell?" he scratched his head and got up moving towards me. I backed up a bit so I would still be in clear view. He sat back down, and I followed him back, still spinning. "Is this real?" he mumbled.

I changed my motion to up and down, *Yes*.

That gave him a start. I went back to the circle. He looked at the beer in his hand and said, "Only had half, I can't be drunk."

I went up and down. *Yes*.

"I must be dreaming."

Side to side. *No.*

That seemed to do it. "My name is Nate," he said slowly and clearly to me.

Yes.

"I am dreaming."

No.

"What are you?"

I spun in a circle, Yes/No wouldn't work. Nate being a non-dummy, he got it.

"Yes, no. You can only answer yes, no questions?"

Yes.

"Holy shit!" He got up and began pacing, kicking debris out of his way. I stayed in front of him spinning in a circle keeping in his field of vision.

He stopped, and reached out his hand to touch the light that was me. I am not sure why, but I kept out of his grasp. He shivered, and went out into the night. The moon wasn't up yet, and the night was dark with the glow of Tucson in one direction, the dim glow of Phoenix in the other, and a few stars visible above.

I kept with him, staying in his field of vision.

"Leave me alone."

No.

"What are you?" he repeated. "Right, yes or no. Twenty questions." He stopped speaking for a bit, his brow furrowed. "OK, you are intelligent and you want to communicate with me."

Yes.

"OK, here's the deal: I am going back inside, you stay here, I'll be right back." I bobbed up and down and stayed put as he went back into the trailer.

He came back with his phone and a bottle of Tequila. He took a pull on the bottle, pointed the phone at me and took a picture.

"Holy shit!!" he yelled looking at the picture his phone had taken, "You are real." He plopped down into a cheap folding chair and gaped at me, the phone falling from his grasp. I went over and looked. The picture showed a fuzzy and small, but unmistakable, blob of light. It wouldn't hold up as any kind of evidence, but it did prove he had seen something.

We spent the next hour, until he passed out, in a bizarre game of twenty questions. Are you an alien? Do you mean me harm? Do you want a drink?—this when he was pretty far gone. And lots I couldn't answer: Why me? What are you? What do you want?

It was frustrating. Soon he was sprawled in that chair unconscious and he hadn't asked one question that I could use to get him down the right path.

Transmission #47
Received 2010/12/13 02:40:16

After Tamara told me how her fiancé John died, she really opened up to me about SECI. It took a while for her to get it out, but it all became clear. The wound she carried; the driving need to communicate with the dead; her hijacking of Jin's EM shielding research; all of it.

In some ways she was stuck in the denial stage of grief. The SECI project was a huge leap: a Hail Mary, really. Starting with nothing but the unsubstantiated, superstition-riddled mythology about ghosts to go on. Yeah, that was a hell of a leap.

At least that is what I thought until she told me about her haunting.

Here's the thing about the unexplained: it is easy to take it and mold it to your existing beliefs, to use it to support what you want to believe. Just ask any conspiracy nut about 9/11. Go ahead, I dare you. Or Google it and see what you find. There are plenty of odd facts that have been stitched together to paint a picture of a government that allowed 9/11 to happen to suppress the people (the Patriot Act, unwarranted wiretapping, extraordinary rendition, etc.). And I am not saying I know the truth, just that facts are being used to support a conclusion, not to find the truth.

So, when you look at a series of unexplained events, filtered through the notoriously unreliable human brain, that is in the midst of serious grieving, you find it easy to dismiss most things that "ghosts" do. You know, if ghosts were real, why isn't there truly incontrovertible evidence? (And yes, I am fully aware of the irony of that statement. Me being a ghost and all, producing what is hopefully incontrovertible evidence.)

Another, less long winded way to say all this is: people believe what they want to believe, often in spite of, not because of, the evidence.

When Tam started talking about her haunting, all these things ran through my mind.

"You think I'm crazy," she said. She must have read my face.

"No... No, really I don't. It's just that I've never come across anything even halfway convincing."

"Do you think I came to this conclusion lightly?" she asked. "I am an engineer, for God's sake; we just don't jump to conclusions. I denied what was happening for the longest time, but the incidents just kept happening."

It was small things at first. Every time she turned on the TV it would be on ESPN. John had loved ESPN, but she never watched it after he died, she actively avoided it. She dismissed it as a quirk of the TV, and after a while just stopped turning it on all together.

She was having trouble sleeping, plagued by recurring nightmares about the night John died. At the end of the dream John was again on the sidewalk bleeding trying to talk to her about something, and just as he started to speak she woke up. It seemed that every time this happened it was 1:16 or 3:20. John was born on January 16th (1/16) and she and John had planned to marry on March 20th (3/20). This she dismissed as a psychological quirk, that she was probably waking up at lots of different times but just remembered those two. To prove the hypothesis she kept a digital camera by her bed and every time she woke from one of the nightmares, she took a picture. Sure enough, every time it was either 1:16 or 3:20. It still might be psychological, but if it was, it was mighty deep. She started to get concerned.

What happened with the radio was much harder to explain away. One day while she was driving to campus the radio turned itself on while "Just the Two of Us" was playing. It was kind of their song and it started playing at: *Darling, when the morning comes / And I see the morning sun / I want to be the one with you.* She had to pull over, it made her cry so hard. If this had happened once, she could have dismissed it, but it happened six times over a three week period. The radio would come on, tuned to a different station each time, and the song would start on those same lyrics.

She questioned her sanity then. Was she imagining it? This just wasn't possible was it? She began using her cell phone to record as she drove her car. She needed to make sure she wasn't imagining it. She wasn't. The recordings verified it. This, for her, was evidence. Not the kind of thing that would hold up to serious scrutiny (you could easily say it was a hoax, that she had turned on the radio, or created the recording), but it was enough for her. Something was going on.

A few more phenomena occurred too: lights turning themselves on and off; whispers in her ear she couldn't quite explain; and odd unexplainable lights floating in the apartment over John's favorite chair.

After that she started believing and started trying to find a way to achieve clearer communications with him. She read every book on the afterlife she could find and went to every psychic in the area.

The books didn't sit well with her engineering mind, and neither did the psychics. Nowhere could she find the consistency and repeatability she needed. The books contradicted each other, and so did the psychics. Some psychics just seemed to pull out convenient phrases that everyone could see their loved one in: "He wants you to know that he is OK"; "He wants to make sure you know he loves you"; "He's sorry about how he left things"; "He wishes it could have been different." She admitted that these things were comforting to hear, but not what she really needed. Some psychics seemed to come up with some remarkable facts about her (the biking accident that produced the scar under her lip; her childhood obsession with horses; and John's inability to sit through a romantic comedy), but when she tried to find out what he was trying to tell her when he died, no one came up with anything useful.

One night in the bathtub after months on this quest, the idea for SECI just popped into her head. There had to be a logical way to explain the ghostly phenomena, and EM radiation fit for some of it. How else could ghosts be sometimes seen and (apparently) photographed? They had to emit visible light. She knew Jin and that he was working on EM shielding and EM detection and that he needed help. She got out of the tub right then and there and called Jin, and lobbied him relentlessly until he allowed her to join the project and add the SECI component.

"So, do you expect him to hop in that chamber and start talking to you when it is done?" I asked after she had revealed the last of the story to me.

"No," she said with a sigh. "The haunting phenomenon only lasted about a month. If it was him, he is probably long gone by now."

"Then why?"

"I *have* to know."

"Know what?"

"If ghosts are real. If life goes on beyond this mortal form. I have to know. I can't explain it any better than that."

And really she didn't need to. I got it. I understood.

Transmission #48
Received 2010/12/13 04:10:25

Not long after dawn, Nate roused himself enough to stumble into the trailer and get himself into his bed. That afternoon when he woke up again, he came back out, found his phone, looked at the picture, and muttered, "Holy shit!"

He was different that day, just a little bit. He kept looking at the picture and muttering to himself. He was a touch more cordial to his clients.

We did it again that night. I didn't have to turn off the flat-screen, because he never turned it on. He plopped himself onto that chair outside the trailer and ate his dinner in the dark, clearly waiting for me.

Once again, he didn't ask me any useful questions. He took more pictures, got quickly drunk, and became more interested in making me doing things: "Fly in a square," "Now a triangle," "Get right next to me while I take a picture of myself."

Shortly before he passed out he said, "I wish JJ was here to see this."

I bobbed madly up and down, but he didn't get it.

"You too? You wish JJ was here to see this?"

I kept going up and down, "no" didn't seem like a good answer.

"He was a good friend and I miss him, let's drink to JJ." He took a long pull on the bottle and splashed some in my direction. He started pacing, going on about how he missed me, and telling stories of our friendship (which was very hard for me to be witness to). His speech becoming more slurred and incoherent until he passed out on the ground.

The next night I tried something different. When he got the bottle out, I flew to it, touching the top and moved from side to side.

"You don't want me to drink?"

Yes.

"OK, what do you want?"

I moved from the bottle to the trailer door bobbing around rapidly. Nate got it, and followed me into the trailer, leaving the bottle. I then went to the door of the guest bedroom and bobbed there.

"You want me to go in there?"

YES.

He paused, his face going slack, "Why?" I couldn't answer that so I bobbed in front of the door as if knocking. He sighed and opened the door. I flew over to a picture of Nate and Me at the Grand Canyon that hung on the wall. I went to the part of the picture with me and bobbed at it.

"JJ?"

YES.

"Yes, that is JJ?" his tone tumbled, "That *was* JJ."

I went back and forth furiously. *NO! NO!*

"What? JJ died."

I moved the light back and forth again: *NO.*

"Yes he did, I don't understand." And it hit me, now that Nate was doing things for me, I didn't have to use yes/no. I flew out, over to his laptop and bobbed at the lid.

He followed, opening it. I tried to land the "I" key with my light, but it was too big, so I shrunk my light down to the size of a dime and then landed on the "I" key.

"I?" Nate asked.

I moved to the space bar, then to "A," "M," and the space bar again.

"'I am'! Holy shit! You're typing!?"

YES!

I continued and hit "j," went up and came back down on "j." Nate repeated the letters after me.

"'JJ.' 'I am JJ'—Holy fuck!" His hands went to his head, his breath came in gasps. "Holy shit! JJ is that you?"

YES! YES! YES!

Interview Transcript
Janet Lynch / Nate Luca: Part 9

Janet: Oh my God, Nate! Why didn't you tell me any of this?

Nate: I... I was ashamed.

Janet: Of JJ communicating with you?

Nate: No. Of how far I had fallen, and how far I had yet to go.

Janet: What do you mean?

Nate: Just wait. We're getting there.

Tamara: So you can confirm the communication.

Nate: Yes.

Tamara: Can we get a copy of the pictures you took?

Nate: Yes.

Transmission #49
Received 2010/12/14 02:21:56

I would like to tell you that after I got through to Nate that night, everything was smooth sailing from there. It wasn't. Life (and death) in my experience is rarely that simple. Humans are complicated; "Happily Ever After" is just for stories.

I didn't "type" much more than that—it had been many days since I had faded and I was beat. I signed off, "*NEED REST CUL.*" I let the world fade.

When I came to it was dark and I was at Nate's place, but he wasn't there, the tow truck was gone too. I flew up to his roof and worked on a better, less taxing, way to "glow." I took one hand, and tried to vibrate just it into the visible spectrum. It took a while, but I got it so that only my hand was involved in "glowing," and I could control the size and intensity of the glow. It was, once I figured it out, easier to do—both physically (if you can call it that) and physiologically. I felt more myself when just the one hand was changed, not my entire form.

When Nate got home we started up our conversation. He

sat down with his food and a beer, turned on the laptop and opened a word processor, as I "glowed" by a key he would press it, my words forming on the screen.

"Is it really you JJ?"

Y.

He looked a little sheepish and said, "Prove it. Sorry, but I got to make sure this is not some kind of joke."

I had trouble seeing how this could be a joke, but I typed anyway, *U SAVED ME FROM ARTY.*

"Yeah, yeah I did, but that's pretty well known."

I thought for a second, I needed something good. *LOST UR VIRGINITY TO CINDY M IN—*

"OK, OK, I am sold. Enough." He was silent for a while, his brow scrunched in thought. "So what is it like?"

BEING DEAD?

"Yeah, what is the other side like?"

DONT THINK I AM THERE YET.

"Well, where you are, is it bad?"

IT IS EVERYTHING KINDA LIKE LIFE.

We chatted like this for a while; I told him bits about what it was like being dead. It is an odd way to communicate, he could talk so fast, but it took time for us to type my answers. Often he would ask me several questions at once, making it difficult to answer him.

Once he opened his fourth beer I typed, *REMEMBER AFTER MY DAD DIED WHAT I WAS LIKE.*

"It was hell bro."

I NEEDED HELP.

"Yeah, it was like pulling teeth to give it to you."

NOW U NEED HELP. That shut Nate up; he walked outside, ending our conversation. I didn't follow him, I knew he needed time.

We didn't "talk" until the next evening, when I brought up the same topic. *I NEEDED HELP U WOULDNT GIVE UP.*

Nate let out a big sigh and took a drink of his beer. "I know where you're going."

I WILL NOT GIVE UP EITHER.

"JJ, I... It's hard man, so hard."

I WILL NOT GIVE UP.

"I know, and I'm so glad to talk to you, but you know it is not the same."

I KNOW IT SUCKS.

"Sucks bad." Nate left the laptop and flopped down on the couch flipping through channels. I let him be. I knew Nate well enough to know this would take time. I waited until he went to bed (he got pretty drunk, but didn't pass out—progress), and flew off to the university.

All the typing we had been doing got me to thinking about Tam and Jin and their SECI Chamber.

Transmission #50
Received 2010/12/14 03:01:25

The lab looked the same: the "chamber" on one side, desks and displays on the other. Jin had given me a good tour when we had finished, so I knew what was what.

Being in the lab as a ghost brought new meaning to the posters hanging on the walls: X-Files, "The Truth is Out There"; Ghost Busters and Ghost Busters Two; and the movie poster for "Ghost," of course. I never asked, but I am sure it was Jin who did this; just his sense of humor and his way at playfully jabbing at Tam. Well, there wouldn't be any more cause for jokes soon.

I was most interested in the read-outs showing EM activity in the chamber. It was scrolling on a large flat-screen mounted on the wall, a large display of current activity (last fifteen minutes), and a smaller one of the last hour, and a small graph along the bottom of the last twenty-four hours. There was nothing there, not a thing, just a flat line like on my EKG when they were trying to revive my crushed body.

I was proud of Tam and Jin, they had done it. Light, easy to work with EM shielding, I hope it makes them rich.

But now it was time for phase two of SECI. I was an extra-corporeal, intelligent (some would say), and knowledgeable about the project. It was time to try it out.

I walked through the chamber wall into the center. It felt different in there, somehow quiet—I liked it. It was evenly lit. Light is, of course, EM radiation. The chamber did not detect light, it was easy to block so it wasn't relevant to the experiment. Jin had told me they left it lit so the ECs could read the instructions, not that he was sure whether they would need light or not.

I looked over the chamber, at the panels with the symbols engraved above the letter or punctuation they represent. In the center of the engravings was a small feedback display. This display, as well as the lights, was driven by fiber optics, so only light entered the chamber, no other EM radiation.

Vowels were based on a circle: an "e" was a simple circle; an "a" was the circle with a smaller circle (or dot) to the right; an "i" was the circle with a dot to the left and the right.

Consonants were more complex, there were four series of letters: "BCDFG," "HJKLM," "NPQRS," and "TVWXYZ." Each series was based on a basic shape: square, rectangle, triangle, and half-circle, with added dots for each of the variants. Punctuation had another basic shape and variants too.

Simple enough, but there were a lot of shapes to master. That first night I spent a few hours on "e." With Nate I had figured out how to use just my hand to form a shape and to radiate at a different frequency.

I had a fright about it before I really started: what if the chamber could detect me as soon as I entered? I went back into the lab and was relieved to find that, no, it hadn't. The display was still a flat-line. This confirmed, for me, that a ghost's natural emanation is a very high frequency, higher than the chamber was able to detect.

I went back in, turned my left hand into a circle (I always was a lefty), and lowered the vibration of just my hand. After about a minute I got it down into a frequency that registered; a large "e" popped up on the display.

What now? That was hard enough, how do I tell it to do another "e"? I let the frequency come back up, and the big "e" disappeared, and a smaller one showed on the bottom of the display. I lowered my frequency, and another big "e" came up again, raised it and there were two "e"s on the bottom of the display.

I was at this for a while; I found it very taxing to constantly change the vibration of my hand. So, on a whim after an "e" had formed, I plunged my hand through the wall of the chamber where I hoped the EM radiation would be blocked. Sure enough another "e" appeared on the line display. I pulled it out and a new big "e" appeared. This was a definite improvement.

I went out into the lab, and saw what I had done on the big display. Spike after spike of activity on the fifteen minute graph with a small letter "e" above most of the spikes.

I knew this would baffle Tam and Jin, but I was tired and couldn't do more. I faded right then and there.

Transmission #51
Received 2010/12/14 03:59:16

I came to back at Nate's place just as he was being called out on his first tow. I rode with him for his shift, and later we talked a little. After Nate had passed out, I went to the university and practiced in the chamber.

This became a pattern that went on for about a week.

Nate and I would talk, but not much. I was relentless in telling him that he needed help. Small talk didn't interest me, and Nate wasn't much interested in getting help. Some nights we would talk longer, when Nate was open, some nights hardly at all. Progress was happening; at least I had convinced myself of that, so I kept at it.

My progress in the chamber was much more rewarding. I mastered all the basic shapes, and could pretty quickly type ABHNT. I progressed from there to mastering all the shapes with their dot variants and getting comfortable transforming from one to another.

I could then start to type, and did some silly messages like "JJ WAS HERE," "JJ LIVES," "HI TAM AND JIN, THIS IS JJ." I quickly found that, just like with keyboarding, I made a lot of mistakes. It was also clear that my writing looked like hell without punctuation, so I mastered those shapes, and started to write what you are reading now.

The going was so slow at first that I went back to experimenting. I was typing, essentially, with one finger, slow and not fun. So I trained my right hand, and then my left foot, and then my right foot to create the shapes. Not as good as ten fingers, but much better than one hand. I was tempted to create more limbs, but I heeded Banquo's training and kept it to the four. It was a big strain on my form anyway, and quite exhausting.

I created a rhythm. My left leg, the one I had the most trouble with, I always kept as an "e." I would queue up letters on the other three limbs, and pull them out of the chamber's shielding when they were ready. It meant I was holding four shapes at once, with up to two changing at once, but it made the process bearable. Like I said, it is an exhausting process.

Hopefully Tam and Jin have edited out the false starts; this whole thing should begin with: "When someone dies, the world doesn't stop."

Transmission #52
Received 2010/12/14 04:45:19

After my week of training in the chamber, Nate and I had come to an impasse: he would no longer talk to me. The last night we talked I typed, *CALL MA SHE IS WORRIED.*

"JJ, I can't."

U NEED THE KIND OF HELP SHE GOT ME.

His big shoulders slumped and he said, "Nothing will ever make this right."

YES BUT IT CAN B BETTER THAN THIS.

"What's wrong with this?!" Nate said, his arms encompassing the mess around him.

GRIEF IS HARD I AM IN IT 2.

He didn't reply, his mouth held tight, so I said, *I LOST MY BEST FRIEND 2.*

Nate's face fell, it looked like he was about to cry when he surged up, threw the door open, and went out into the desert night.

"Go JJ, just go. I don't need you nagging me. I will do this the way I do this. Just go!"

I had followed him out, letting my light get bigger.

I honored his request and left. I made a point of moving my light down the road for a while so he could tell I was going before I dispensed with the light and flew to the university— at least there I could accomplish something.

Nate and I have never fought much. Once in high school when we both went after the same girl (who ultimately went for a football player, of course), and after my dad died and Rhiannon left. Honestly we are not very good at it. We get along so well so much of the time that it is foreign territory.

I kept up my routine with him, but stayed out of sight and just watched. I was waiting for him to make the first move, say something so I knew he wanted to talk—he was probably doing the same.

That all changed the day Ma came to visit.

Interview Transcript
Janet Lynch / Nate Luca: Part 10

Janet: Nate, why didn't—

Nate: (holding hands up) I can confirm the accuracy of this. That is all I have to say.

Transmission #53
Received 2010/12/15 01:16:26

It was around noon when Ma and Jean showed up. I had just arrived and Nate was finishing up a bowl of cereal. She pulled up in her '89 Ford Focus, driving it slowly down the dirt road.

She looked better than when I had seen her last, which felt good. I knew it was hard, but she appeared to be progressing. Jean looked nervous, Ma probably dragged her along for moral support. Going out of your way to face grief is a hard thing to do.

Nate froze in the door when he saw them, milk dripping down his chin, the cereal bowl clutched in his hand.

"Something wrong with your phone?" Ma asked.

"Ahh... No, ma'am," Nate answered timidly.

"You don't consider me family anymore?"

"No! No, ma'am." Nate looked scared. He opened the door most of the way and said, "Do you want to come in?" It was clear he was hoping for a "no."

"What do you think? It's quite a drive." Ma was angry, that was easy to tell, but she was scared too and trying to mask it with bluster.

Nate let them in and quickly brushed trash off the couch so Ma and Jean would have a place to sit.

"Nice place," Jean said with a smirk. Ma glared at her.

After they sat, Ma looked him up and down and said, "You look like hell Nate."

"Yes ma'am," Nate said again.

Ma's eyes narrowed as her gaze took in the whole of the living room. "I'm worried about you. This... This thing—"

"I know," Nate said, "JJ... I... I have never lost someone so close to me."

"Surviving is a bitch, ain't it?"

Nate's eyebrows shot up, "Yes ma'am!"

"But what else can you do?"

His face fell and he said, "I don't know."

"Nate, you need to do better than this."

Nate paused, his head down and quietly said, "I know."

"You need help."

Nate nodded his head.

Ma got up, took a piece of paper out of her purse and pressed it into Nate's hand. "This is the lady that helped JJ, she is expecting you at 1 p.m. tomorrow."

"Yes ma'am."

"Good!" Ma said. "Jean, what are you doing sitting there? Grab a trash bag, we have work to do."

They leapt into action, Ma ordering Jean and Nate around and within the hour the trailer was in respectable shape.

Nate was hauling the last bag of garbage out when his phone rang. He took the call and went back in. "There's been a big wreck on the 10," he said, "I gotta go."

"OK Nate. You keep that appointment."

"I will," Nate said. "The wreck is east of here blocking both directions. You might as well stay put for a while, I'll call when it clears."

"Thanks dear." Nate headed towards the truck. "Be careful Nate," Ma called after him, "it's Halloween—people get weird."

I was torn, I wanted to spend time with my mother, but I wasn't convinced by Nate's fast turnaround. I lingered for a moment and saw Ma collapse on the couch crying. With her head in her hands she said to Jean, "Thank God he didn't make that hard, I couldn't have borne it if he had."

I raced off and caught up with Nate. I knew he had no intention of keeping that appointment. He had agreed so quickly to spare Ma.

Transmission #54
Received 2010/12/15 02:10:43

Halloween, "All Hallows' Eve." I didn't know much about it before I died, not beyond the costumed, candied fun. But hang around a graveyard in late October with a bunch of ghosts and you'll get an ear full.

They say that the veil is thin on Halloween. The dead grow more powerful, and the living can often see beyond the veil, into our world. It is the one day of the year that death and all things dark and superstitious are actually embraced.

There is also Día de los Muertos (Day of the Dead) on November 2nd—which Jesus has filled us all in on—celebrated in Mexico. They really get to the heart of it, asking the dead to come visit, saying prayers for them, leaving them trinkets and food. And they make a party of it—telling funny stories, drinking and dancing. I'd love to be around for one of those celebrations.

Either way you cut it, things do tend to get strange during this time of year. For my part, I can say that I felt stronger that night than I had ever before, and did things I might not otherwise have been capable of doing (or surviving).

When I caught up with him, Nate was almost to the end of the dirt road. He was different; his energy was palpable, wound tight, manic-like. This wasn't good.

He turned off the dirt road, onto the service road and was soon barreling east on I-10. He had a grin on his face when he said, "JJ, I got this figured out, it's going to be OK."

His tone, his look, terrified me. Grief is a process; it doesn't turn on a dime like that. He had something in mind, and I was too scared to even imagine it.

When we hit traffic Nate started flashing his lights and moved onto the left shoulder. We eased past the half mile of stopped vehicles and were on site less than ten minutes after we left.

The accident was a mess. At this point I-10 is two divided lanes in each direction with a small median in between. A semi, with three trailers (one of those highway trains) in the right lane had apparently plowed into a couple cars in the left lane (maybe a steering malfunction!?). One car had flipped and lay on its side in the median, the other (a crushed mess) ended up going all the way through the median, and plowing into oncoming traffic. The semi driver had overcorrected, turning right, and had jackknifed the truck. It had turned on its side and several more cars had run into this mess. In all, the semi and six other cars were involved in the eastbound lanes, and about four cars in the westbound.

Some people had gotten out of their cars and were trying to help the survivors out, but no police or ambulances had arrived yet. With Nate's location, he was often the first on the scene for wrecks like this.

Nate grabbed one of those auto escape tools (a combo hammer and seatbelt cutter) and hopped out of the truck, a spring in his step. He went from car to car making sure those that wanted, and were able, got out. He smashed windows, cut seat belts, dragged people away. He was this huge hulking force with such intent that others wondering what to do looked to him for instructions.

In some ways this was the Nate I knew, I had been in these situations with him before. He was fearless and moved quickly. For a moment my worries eased.

I followed him to the new Toyota Prius on its side in the median; the calls for help from it drawing him there. He peered through the windshield and saw a woman with a bleeding head struggling to get out. He climbed up on the car, told the woman to cover her face, smashed the window and dropped down next to her.

"It's gonna be OK, ma'am," Nate said.

"My baby! My baby!" the woman cried.

Nate looked at the back seat and blanched at the site: the child was quiet, and its head hung at an unnatural angle.

When I looked I saw the body, but I saw something else too. The baby's spirit was hovering over its body, a silver cord reaching back to it. It was crying out and reaching for its mother.

Shit! I had no idea what to do. The baby was dead, but suffering.

"Ma'am, we've got to get you out of here," Nate said as he wedged himself in above the woman and started kicking at the shattered windshield. After a few blows the windshield fell out. He then pulled away her deployed air bags, cut off her seatbelt and pulled her out.

While he did that, I panicked. What could I do to help? After Nate took the mother away the baby began to wail, a piercing, eerie sound. Its cord was short and it could not follow its mother. I wanted to follow Nate, but was riveted by this infant's pain. "It's OK, it's going to be OK," I said, the baby's wail growing in intensity.

Banquo, Banquo, he would know what to do. With that wail feeding my panic I cried out "Banquo!" briefly drowning out the baby.

I looked back to Nate; he had dragged the woman to the side of the road and was commandeering a bystander, telling him to help her, and to not let her go back to her car. I got a glimpse of the man Nate was instructing. He was half Nate's mass and quickly agreed.

I looked back to the baby and was trying to calm it when I heard a voice behind me say, "JJ, is everything OK?"

I jumped, literally, right out of the car. I know I had just called for him, but hearing him like that scared the hell out of me. "Banquo?"

"At your service." He seemed his usual calm self around the chaos of the living, the dying, and the dead.

"This baby, it needs help."

We both went into the car, Banquo looking over the situation. He looked at the baby and its wailing ghost, and then looked back at me, his eyes narrowing. I think he was going to tell me what to do, but thought better of it, "I'll take care of the baby. Go see if you can find someone else to help."

"How?"

"The same way you helped Anna-Beth and your mother."

"OK," I answered.

"JJ. Listen to me," Banquo said, staring into my eyes, "you know what to do. You can handle this."

"OK," I repeated, this time with some confidence. I turned to look over the situation.

"And JJ."

"What?"

"Get dressed, it will help."

I looked down and my form was in tatters, nearly transparent. I took a few moments to bring it in and solidify it.

I caught a glimpse of Nate climbing onto the wreck of the semi. Gas was pouring out of the tank. In the distance I heard sirens.

I flew over, the driver was dead, so Nate moved on. The driver's spirit was standing in front of the truck staring at his body.

I firmed up my form even further tapping into the warmth and approached him. "Hi," I said.

"Huh!?" he jumped back.

"It's OK," I said trying to soothe him. "Everything is OK."

"You... you can see me?"

"Yes, just be calm, everything is OK."

"How can you see me, I'm dead?"

"I am dead too. My name is JJ." I extended my hand feeling the warmth growing. He took it and I could see him visibly relax a bit. After we shook hands I put my other hand on his shoulder and gently steered him away from the wreck out towards the desert. His cord was short, so I moved him slowly, gently stretching it out as we walked.

"You're dead?" he asked.

"That I am; it's not so bad."

"I'm dead?"

"Yes sir, you are."

Behind us the semi exploded and people screamed. I didn't know it yet, but that explosion had created more work for both emergency teams (the living and the dead that is).

"What was that?" he asked.

"Nothing to worry about," I assured him.

We went on like that, he was clearly in shock. I just kept my hand on his shoulder pumping him full of all the warmth I could, and keeping the wreck out of his site.

Behind us the emergency vehicles arrived. I just kept talking to him.

After about fifteen minutes he seemed calm, almost normal. His name was Jerry Engle; he was on the end of a long haul trying to make it to Tucson to be with his family.

He turned to me and said, "Do you hear that?"

"What?" I asked. I didn't hear anything beyond the sirens, groans, moans, and shouts.

"Well I don't know if I am hearing it, but it is wonderful."

"Good, good," I said, not knowing what he was talking about, "go with it."

His eyes got this far away look, a smile grew on his face and he was gone. Just gone. I had seen ghosts fade, and that is not what he did. I had seen spirits "pop," and it has a distinctive popping sound. This was just gone.

I looked back to the scene and saw Banquo talking to another new ghost and behind him Nate loading up a car onto his truck.

As I walked towards Banquo, his ghost was suddenly gone too.

"How's the baby?" I asked.

"She moved on."

"Where are they going?"

Banquo shrugged, "Don't know."

"Huh?" How could he not know?

He stopped, looking me over and said, "On. JJ, they went on. To heaven, to hell, purgatory, oblivion, reincarnation—take your pick."

"You mean—"

"We don't have time for this," Banquo cut me off. "There is work to do. Get to it, we will talk later."

I went back in and helped another two ghosts to move *on*. A few more were bardo-brained, and a lost cause at this point.

I wanted to talk to Banquo more about what had happened, but Nate was almost done, and I didn't want to lose him. I flew over there and saw that he had blood on his t-shirt and a big smile on his face.

The car he had loaded had been one of the least damaged ones—it was caved in right front side. The passengers, a man and a woman, had refused medical care and had climbed into the back of his cab.

In a few minutes we were around the accident and heading east into Tucson.

Transmission #55
Received 2010/12/15 04:20:16

Nate hauled the car to Morty's Garage, the first AAA approved place as we headed east. After dropping the car and his passengers off, he headed back to the accident for another car. One lane had opened up in westbound traffic, but aside from that the scene was pretty much the same. Traffic had backed up in both directions for miles and westbound, while moving, was just a trickle. There were some big wreckers there working on getting the semi, and the other totaled cars off to the side of the road so they could get an eastbound lane opened up.

Banquo was still there working with some of the bardo-brains. While Nate loaded his second car I went over to Banquo and asked, "What can I do?"

He sighed, "Not much help for these, not here anyway. If they get dragged along to the morgue I might be able to jostle them out of it there—too much chaos here."

"Do you mind if I ask you a question then?"

"No."

"Did you hear me calling you?"

"Calling?"

"Yeah, I shouted for you, right before you got here."

Banquo chuckled, "Just a fine coincidence my boy. I was at the 911 dispatch office when the call about the accident came in, and I headed right out."

"So, is this what you do?"

"This?"

"Yeah, this?" I said indicating the scene around us—fire engines, ambulances, crushed cars, bleeding people, ghosts, corpses. "I mean besides trying to teach bums like me and Jesus. Is helping others "on" what you do?"

He stopped beaming the warmth at the bardo-brains and faced me. "Yes."

I was taken aback for a moment; a simple clear answer was not what I expect from Banquo. Hoping for more of the same I asked, "Why?"

He paused, his face going briefly slack as if a shadow were passing over it, before saying, "Because it needs to be done."

"Have you felt it? That thing they seem to feel before they go?" I asked, indicating what the semi driver talked about right before he disappeared.

"Yes."

"But you didn't move on?"

"No."

"Why not?"

"I didn't want to."

We went on like that for a while. Banquo was in an answering mood, and I took advantage of it. Well, as much as I could. His answers were curt and to the point, going no further than I asked. Banquo hadn't moved on because he felt like he had work to do here. The *Call*, as he put it, can be refused. It comes back from time to time when you are *ready*.

It was kind of like talking about gravity. Yeah, that gravity, it is the big mysterious force we don't quite understand but it holds the universe together. You can observe it, you can measure it, but it is the kind of force you can never really understand. What Banquo was telling me about life and death was very much like that: a force of nature—observable, describable, measurable, but not understandable.

"Sorry my boy, but it is time we end this discussion," Banquo said.

"But, I am—"

He held his hand up, cutting me off and pointed to Nate's truck moving off.

"Right. Thanks." I flew off and joined Nate.

Interview Transcript
Janet Lynch / Nate Luca: Part 11

Nate: (to Tamara) You want me to comment?

Tamara: Please.

Nate: For my part, everything described is accurate. It must be clear by now that I believe JJ wrote this. I have no doubt.

Tamara: Thank you.

Nate: Can we keep this moving please? Best do it quick or I'll lose my nerve.

Janet: Nate, what?

Nate: Just keep listening, we are almost there.

Transmission #56
Received 2010/12/16 03:05:32

We went back, and Nate hauled one more car off. By this time, traffic was flowing down one lane in both directions and all the injured had been tended to and taken away.

Nate called Ma, telling her traffic was starting to move, but it would be a long wait, and that they were welcome to stay at his house as long as they liked.

I watched him close while he talked to her; his expression became contrite and his shoulders slumped. Once he got off the phone, his face hardened, and his shoulders squared. He was psyching himself up for something, but what?

After hauling the third car away, he stopped at a little taco stand not far off the freeway. He walked up to the window, his face dirty, his shirt stained with blood.

"Shit Nate, what the hell?" said Manny who owned the place and worked it most days.

Nate looked down; he must have forgotten what he looked like. "Ah, this blood ain't mine—big pileup on the 10."

"You wanna borrow a shirt?"

"No, got an extra in the truck, be right back." Nate went to the truck, pulled off the blood stained shirt, and put on a grease stained one. "This better?" he asked when he came back.

Manny smiled and nodded.

Nate ordered some food, bummed some paper off of Manny and sat down at one of the two tables in the place. He started to write on the paper with his shaky print, his big hands lacking the precision to write neatly: "What if you knew that death was not the end? Would you do things different? Would you go on struggling in this life?"

Shit! This was bad. Nate was going to try to join me. For a moment, I felt happy, welcoming this. Nate and I back together and knocking heads on the other side! It had its appeal. Life goes on, whether you're dead or not, so why did it matter if he was on that side, or this side?

That thought didn't stay around long. It was heartily chased away with a big dose of guilt. I had witnessed the devastation death produces, contemplated all that I had lost, and been to the bardo and back twice. This was no picnic over here, and no solution to your troubles on the other side. Yeah, life goes on, but so do your problems.

"I have seen the light," Nate continued to write, "and I know that this is not the end. I *truly* know. One day or another we all die, no one gets out of that. So, why not me, why not today?"

The food came, and Nate ate it quickly washing it down with a couple of Coronas, hoisting the last sip and saying a toast to Uncle Sal. After he ate he continued writing. "So all that stuff about the dead not being gone? Well it's true, so don't grieve for me. I will know if you do."

Nate folded the paper and stuffed it into his back pocket.

He took out all the cash in his wallet (about $50) and left it on the table.

"Thanks Manny," he said with a wave as he headed out to the truck.

I was desperate, how could I stop him? As he climbed into the cab I tried to think of a way to keep the truck from starting, but I couldn't figure out how. I was good at turning things on that were off, but not the other way around. The sun was setting as the truck rumbled to life and he got back on I-10 heading west.

How would I do it? That was the best thought I had: How would *I* do it? I followed that line of thinking, hoping it would get me close to what Nate was thinking.

I would want it to be quick, as pain-free as possible, 100% reliable, and not harm anyone in the process. For me, that would be sticking a gun in my mouth and pulling the trigger. If you had the guts to do it, it is pretty damn reliable, and doesn't hurt anyone else in the process (not physically at least).

Just like every boy who grew up in rural Arizona I knew how to shoot a gun. Nate knew, and had one locked away in the shed. It was Uncle Sal's, he used to carry it along with him when he did tows, but Nate had never thought that was necessary. Being Uncle Sal's, the gun was old, simple, and reliable. It was .32 Smith and Wesson No. 2, the kind used in the Civil War.

It was a long drive back, traffic being real slow, and Nate just crawled along with it. He didn't flip on his lights and drive on the shoulder, that wouldn't have been right, that wouldn't have been Nate. He just crawled along with the rest of the traffic.

I wracked my brain the whole time trying to figure out

how I could stop him, and I came up with nothing. The gun was too dense, too physical for me to affect.

I switched tracks and went to trying to communicate. I vibrated for light and started doing the "no" pattern in front of him as he drove. There were a lot of lights coming at him, so I dialed it up as much as I could. I knew he could see me, but he didn't say anything for long minutes. I just kept at it sweeping my light back in forth in front of him until he finally gave in.

"This has to be bro," he said, his voice hard.

No! No!

"Don't worry. I see it now; it doesn't have to be this hard."

After that he wouldn't talk to me, he just kept driving. Ma's car was gone when we drove up to his place; he pulled right in front of the shed leaving his headlights on as he grabbed the keys and got out.

He opened the shed, rummaged around until he found the ammo can it was kept in, and pulled out the gun. The gun was sleek and long, dark grey metal, with a weathered wooden handle. Nate picked it up and hefted it in his hand and then passed it from his right hand to his left and back to his right again. He pulled out a cloth and rubbed it down. He put it down, and paced in front of the shed—back and forth, back and forth.

"Don't do it, Nate," I intoned as I followed him back and forth. "Don't do this. This is not the answer." I emanated a light sweeping horizontally in front of him telling him: *NO, NO, NO.*

He finally stopped in front of the shed letting out a loud sigh like a balloon deflating. "I can't, I just can't," he said slumping to the ground.

I was elated, and shined my light up and down in an excited *YES!*

With the light from the truck, and his head buried in his hands I don't think he saw me.

His phone rang, it was dispatch, and to my surprise he picked it up. There was someone broken down off the highway near Picacho Peak. He paused for just a moment, deciding I guess, and then told dispatch he would be there in twenty.

Interview Transcript
Janet Lynch / Nate Luca: Part 12

Janet: Nate!

Nate: (holding hand up) I will reserve any further comments until we come to the end of this.

Janet: You can't just leave it like that. Why?

Nate: (arms crossed, silent)

Transmission #57
Received 2010/12/17 02:54:12

I was relieved that he hadn't been able to go through with his plan, but terrified that he would try something else. We drove in a thick, heavy silence; I did not try to communicate with him, lost in my own thoughts.

I recalled that day on the playground when Nate pulled big Arty off of me; his sense of justice had caused him to act. "Cause you didn't deserve what you were getting," he had told me. I remembered how he had taken care of his Uncle Sal, pulled people out of wrecked cars, taken home stray dogs, and always held strong to his own sense of what was right and what was wrong.

This was Nate, this was why I loved him. And this was what was killing him now.

And I related. The world is a horribly messy, fucked up, unjust place. And it doesn't stop, it never stops when you need it, never gives you a break to get it all sorted out. And a guy like Nate can take some of this, but I guess what happened to me was too much. It happens to the best of us. When your world gets pulled out from under you it is hard to get your bearings. If it was Nate that had died, and I knew he was well on the other side, I just might be considering suicide too.

If only I could speak to Nate, really communicate with him; I knew I could talk him out of it. But then again if I could really speak to him, I wouldn't be dead and we wouldn't be in this mess.

I remember reading about a study that claimed only about 10% of people have considered suicide. I found that number to be shocking—shockingly low. I mean, seriously! Either the people in this survey were lying, or they hadn't lived any kind of life. Life is full of pain, and illness, and loss; it seems completely rational to me to ponder ending it all occasionally.

Before I knew it, we were there. A Prius Hybrid was on the shoulder, hood up. A lanky fellow stood with his head under the hood. It was dark out here, so there wasn't much to see.

Nate passed them, pulled over to the shoulder, and backed up, getting in position to tow them. He got out and walked over.

I got out too, but froze. I hadn't seen it, but there was a third figure there hovering (shit!) around the man a cord passing from the ghost to the man. This wasn't the man's soul, because he was clearly alive. This was something else.

"So, what seems to be the problem?" Nate asked as he ambled up shining his flashlight onto the exposed engine. The man turned, keeping his hands behind his back. His face was thin, his cheek bones jutting forth, and his eyes sunk back. "Not sure. Not good with cars," he said, his voice thin and reedy.

"No problem; let me take a look."

The man moved back giving Nate room to look under the hood. He turned and I could see he held a gun behind his back.

"Nate!" I yelled. He didn't hear me, but the ghost attached to the man did.

"He's mine! Stay away!" the ghost hissed at me, referring I am sure to the lanky man.

"Hmmm, nothing jumps out," Nate said. "Probably best if I tow you; there is a good garage just over in Picacho."

"Now! Now! Do it now!" the ghost hissed at the lanky man.

The man took the gun, pressing it to the back of Nate's head and said, "Sorry, we have to get moving faster than that." His hands shook.

Nate stiffened briefly; I could almost see the wheels turning in his mind. He slowly backed out from under the hood, the man kept the gun to the base of his head. "Easy... easy... no sudden moves."

Nate, once he got clear of the car, whirled to face the man, a grin on his face. "Or what? You gonna kill me?"

The man, surprised, took a step back, but kept the gun pointed at Nate's head. "I just need your wallet and your keys. Nobody has to get hurt."

"Keys?" Nate said, pulling his keys out of his pocket. "You mean these keys?" He tossed them into the brush on the side of the road.

"Just shoot him," the spirit said into the man's ear, "he wants it. I can see it. Do him a favor."

"Let me guess," Nate said, "you're on your way to score some..." He tilted his head examining the fellow, "...to score some meth. Your car broke down on the way, and you are just this far from full-on withdrawal." He held his forefinger and thumb close together. "The last thing you need is some big lug, like me, getting in your way. That must really piss you off."

The man was clearly confused by Nate's behavior. He stood in front of his car, Nate stood in back of the tow truck haloed by the light coming from the truck.

"See... See..." the ghost intoned, "he wants it, he does. We need to get our fix, just get his money and let's go!"

"Money, give me your money," the man shouted, his hands shaking more now.

"You mean this money?" Nate said as he drew his wallet out of his back pocket and casually tossed it into the brush. "Woops! Sorry."

The man took a step forward, putting the gun to Nate's head. "Damn you!"

"Just pisses you off doesn't it?"

"Yes. God damn you!"

"Makes you want to shoot me, doesn't it?"

I moved behind the man and his attached spirit and to the Prius, a plan was forming. I had no idea what would happen, but there was more than enough juice in those batteries to light me up and let me do something.

Nate kept taunting the man; the ghost also kept egging him on while I took both hands and vibrated them to conduct electricity. I located the mains and waited.

"It's getting worse now, isn't it?" Nate said. "Poor, poor boy."

"What is wrong with you?" the man asked, his hand shaking.

"Kill him!" the spirit hissed.

"You know, I have a spare key in my boot," Nate said.

"Take it off!" the man demanded.

"No. I don't want to," Nate said.

"What the fuck is wrong with you?"

Nate just smiled.

"Shoot him! Shoot him!" the spirit screamed, reaching down with his hands and superimposing them over the man's bony hands. He was modulating them, I could see that, and soon the hands looked to be one.

I was distracted by this display; I had no idea such things were possible. This spirit had attached to a living body, and was now, apparently, forcing him to do something. And it was working; I saw the man's trigger finger begin to slowly pull back, the gun pointed right between Nate's eyes.

I snapped out of it and plunged my hands into the Prius's bright orange high voltage mains. I felt the energy course through me, my form lighting up like the fourth of July. What I had done before had been 120 volt AC, and had been on breakers at about 20 amps. This was about 500 DC volts at about 200 amps. The electricity just poured out of those batteries into me.

Back at the graveyard where AC versus DC had been thoroughly debated, I learned some things I hadn't known. Edison was a proponent of DC. Since DC doesn't transmit very far or very well he saw a future with power plants on every roof belching pollution into the sky. Tesla, on the other hand, with his crazed electrical experiments, sided with AC. Safer and easy to transport over long distances, power generation could be consolidated. DC, as I was learning, was considerably more dangerous.

If what I had done before was like drinking from a water fountain, this was like drinking from a fire hose. The energy was coursing through me, ripping me apart, and I heard what sounded like something tearing—a great shredding sound accompanied by pops and crackles.

The pain was unbearable. I hadn't really felt physical pain since dying, but now I did. An overwhelming cascade of agony coursed through me, as if every pain nerve in a meat body had been turned all the way up at once.

I twisted around and saw the man/ghost's finger slowly pulling on the trigger. The scene was now brightly lit by a lurid and flickering yellow and red light (me). I also heard a high pitched warbling scream (me) along with the pops and hisses (me again).

The spirit turned and saw me, eyes wide and screamed, "Shoot him, shoot him now!" I lurched forward and plunged my flaming hands into the man's back just as gun went off. The energy poured out of me into him, his mouth opening in a scream as his legs buckled.

The gun went off, but because of the man's spasm the bullet missed Nate's head and plunged into his chest. Surprise grew on Nate's face as he fell back, his head meeting the ground with a sharp crack.

The energy continued to pour from me into the man as he writhed on the ground screaming. I tried to pull away but couldn't. The three of us (the man, the ghost, and me) were locked in a quivering mass as the energy flowed.

Soon the ghost tore away from the man, the man's screams growing in pitch, and the ghost disappeared. The man and I stayed locked like that, both of us screaming, shaking and writhing until the energy dissipated.

When it finally stopped, Nate was laid out on the ground, blood flowing out of the bullet wound and pooling around his head where it had smacked the hard ground.

The man laid still and silent on the ground, dead. I had

electrocuted him. Smoke wafted off his clothes and burnt skin as his spirit rose from his body. He stood there looking at the scene in confused wonder, a "what the fuck" forming on his lips.

I am not sure what I looked like, but the light was gone so I was no longer lighting the place up. I felt exploded, ripped up, destroyed, devastated.

I tried to move, but couldn't. I tried to speak, but couldn't. I stayed that way for what seemed like a long, long time with Nate still and the man's ghost wandering around his body mumbling.

I figured I must be dying. I know, I know, I was already dead, right? Well my body was dead, but what I felt like was dying this time was me, the real me. Or maybe what I felt was my form dying, that ghostly body I had been inhabiting. I was filled with shock, regret, and fear. I had killed a man, failed to keep Nate from getting shot, and killed myself in the process

And then I heard it: the Call. The same thing that semi driver must of heard, except it wasn't exactly hearing, or seeing, or feeling, but all of those and none of those—somehow I *sensed* it. It was a sweet invitation like the warmth itself reaching down to me and inviting me in. It sang to me of succor and relief, of an end to the pain, and most especially of redemption.

Did I have a choice? My form was wrecked, my ghost-body dying, could I resist? Did I want to resist? So much was left undone, so many questions. I said—no, not said, but emoted—"No", and the warmth of the Call slowly faded.

I was left there in searing pain, feeling very alone and very afraid. Would it ever ask again? Would I be like this forever? Would Nate survive? What would happen to me now?

Those thoughts raced through my head as the world ever so slowly faded.

Interview Transcript
Janet Lynch / Nate Luca: Part 13

Nate: (to Janet) Please, just don't say anything. Please. (pause) I feel bad enough about this already.

Tamara: Would you say this is accurate?

Nate: Yes. Accurate. Far too accurate.

Janet: I had no idea. That electrical phenomenon that killed that man was JJ?

Nate: (nodding his head yes)

Janet: Oh my God! You could have told me, I would have understood.

Nate: (crying)

Tamara: Jin, cut the cameras, I think we all need a break.

Transmission #58
Received 2010/12/18 01:34:43

You know I think I was ready for an end there, a real end. I think oblivion was at the top of my list—just not to exist anymore, a final and true escape. But I had said "no" to the Call so I wasn't sure what would happen. I was half convinced that my form was so damaged it could no longer support me (a *me* that went beyond my physical body and my ghostly form).

And with what happened next, oblivion was something I often wished for.

I came back in bits and by degrees. The first thing I remember was being back at the graveyard, near my grave I think. Jesus's face came swimming into view.

"Wwaahhh mmmmm," I groaned. I was trying to ask where I was.

"There you are," Jesus said, his face tight. "Someone go get Banquo," he yelled.

I felt crisp, brittle, unplugged—burned out.

The next time I awoke it was to Banquo's face. I could see his hands near me and feel the warmth seeping into me. I tried to speak, but he cut me off saying, "Just rest my boy. This is going to take some doing."

I was in and out like that for days before I became fully conscious. Every time I came to, one of the Circle gang was with me, pumping the warmth into me. Banquo, Jesus, Fredrick, Jim, Jane, Mary, and quite a few others.

When I finally came around enough to talk, I was with Jesus.

"Nate?" I said, my voice a low growl.

"He is alive," Jesus said.

"Ahhhhhhhhh."

"He is out of the hospital in a long-term care facility."

"I. Go. There," I said, feeling like those three words were a marathon.

"Not yet."

"What—" I couldn't get any more out.

"What happened to him? Lots of blood loss by the time he was found, collapsed lung, bad concussion."

"How you know?"

Jesus smiled, "We have been keeping an eye on him for you."

"Thanks."

"No problem," Jesus said.

"Man?"

"The one who died?"

I nodded and asked, "What happened?"

"Sorry, we don't know. We have pieced things together from our time with Nate, but don't really know what happened."

Later, when Banquo was there, I slowly and laboriously told them what had happened. A crowd gathered while I did the telling—a spontaneous Circle gathering. They were all silent, which I was grateful for, with looks of shock, awe, disbelief, and caring on their faces.

When I was done, Banquo nodded his head towards me once, sharply, and turned to the crowd, "You all have a shift, now get moving until it is your turn."

When I was alive I had been real sick, broke my arm, and recovered from many a brawl, but they were all nothing in comparison to this. That electricity had destabilized my form, badly.

Normally life as a ghost is fluid and easy. Your form molds itself to your thoughts. I had what I think was the equivalent of nerve damage, the connection between "me" (a definition I continue to struggle with) and my form was poor, the wires crossed.

Transmission #59
Received 2010/12/18 02:10:21

About a week after waking up I was able to move around again, my form a wispy mess. I was worried about Nate and about Ma, but I didn't have the energy to do anything about it.

Jesus spent a lot of time with me, helping me practice with my form, get control back. I also spent a lot of time alone wandering the graveyard. I needed time to think. Actually, it was more about not thinking. I would wander about and let the memories and the feelings rise, unopposed, and let them wash over me. I really wasn't in shape to offer much resistance: my form was weak, but so was my... my soul, I guess you would say. Surrender was the only available option on both fronts.

And I had to take on another journey of grief and guilt. I had killed a man, and that was not an easy thing to confront. Denial would have been the safest route, but I was too raw, too stretched to manage it.

JJTTSABD #6: *Grief is grief whether you are alive or dead; there is no getting out of grieving what you have to grieve.*

It was a heavy thing, and confusing to me. I had acted to save Nate, and someone else had died in the process. I really couldn't find a way to look at it that didn't put the blame for this mess on me. My contacting Nate had seemed to go well, but it had pushed him over the edge until he viewed suicide as viable and safe. Because of the state he was in, and finding himself unable to take his own life, he actively tried to get the lanky man to shoot him. My desperate attempt to stop the man had killed him.

And after all that, I had heard the Call. What was that about? What about driving my best friend to suicide, killing a man, and frying my form made me suddenly *ready*? Was it better that the man die, and the spirit that was—dare I say it?—possessing him, expelled? Had I somehow been in service of a larger force? And if I was, who the hell came up with such a screwed up plan?

And if I had said "yes" to the Call, what then? Heaven? Hell? Bardo? Oblivion? Reincarnation? Judgment? Redemption? Damnation?

So I walked, and thought, and felt, and just let it roll over me and run its course.

After a week of this I was down in the southeastern end of the graveyard and heard what sounded like a cat coming from the bushes. I went over and saw a black cat wandering around and through the shrubs. It was a big cat, probably ten or twelve pounds, with a crooked ear, intelligent green eyes, and a wandering tail.

I watched it for a while; I found its movements soothing. Soon it noticed me and walked over rubbing itself against my form. That cat was, I now realized, a ghost.

When that cat touched me, I felt it. It felt like a cat. Now that may not seem like a big deal to you, but to me it was a thrill. Since dying, the only sensation of touch I had was when Jesus and I had "touched" hands in my hiding place in William and Anna-Beth's building. But this was on another level; it felt real.

"Hey big fellow," I said to it, "do you belong to Marilyn?"

Motor and I spent the next few hours together as I looked for Marilyn. I found that his presence kind of smoothed things out for me: my mind was calmer, my form sharper, my soul peaceful. I was able to control my form enough to pick him up and pet him.

His purr, that loud rumbling motor of his, felt like the warmth that others had been pouring into me, only different. It was a wilder, stronger version of it. When I was holding Motor and he was happy, everything was right with the world. I now understood why Marilyn was always looking for him.

I found Marilyn that evening around dusk, and handed Motor over. You should have seen her face; she lit up with a smile that was nearly blinding. Giving him up was hard, but the look on her face made it worth it.

"Motor, Motor, where have you been?" she said.

"I found him over in the southeast corner of the graveyard messing around in some bushes."

"Thank you JJ. Thank you," she said as she wandered off, cooing to him.

The Midnight Circle was crucial to my recovery during this period. Forget the Old Globe Theater—Shakespeare is at its best when preformed at midnight, under the open sky, in a graveyard, by a pack of ghosts. Trust me, you can't beat it.

Banquo knew, and the Circle did, a lot of plays besides Shakespeare, but the Bard's tragedies became my favorites—

the death and destruction driven by human greed, lust, and other failings; the worry about death and the afterlife; the supernatural forces at play; the way the old English seeped into my brain without a full knowledge of some of the words and idioms, somehow making the meaning clearer and more impactful. One performance even peeled away one of the layers of mystery surrounding Banquo.

Those of you more attuned to Shakespeare's works may have caught it already, the rest of you probably just realized that Banquo is an awfully odd name (and it fits, he's a pretty odd guy).

As it turns out Banquo is a character in Shakespeare's Macbeth. Excuse me, "The Tragedy of Macbeth." Professor Banquo would want me to use the proper title. Shakespeare's Banquo is a general and an ally of Macbeth and was with him when he met the Three Witches. Macbeth's need to ensure the crown of Scotland drives him to have Banquo murdered. Banquo subsequently haunts Macbeth.

Banquo, of course, played his namesake in the Midnight Circle rendition of the play—he didn't have many lines, but the character is present in human and ghost form throughout much of the play. While playing a ghost, Banquo, for the first time, relaxed his form and let it go wispy, truly looking like a ghost.

I was dying (not literally of course) to know why he had done this; why he had changed his name. "So, *Banquo*?" I asked after the play was over and the Midnight Circle had broken up.

"So, *JJ*?" he replied.

"Oh come on! You know what I mean."

"Perhaps, but if you have a question why don't you just ask it?"

"OK. Why did you take the name Banquo? It's not your real name; it can't be."

He paused for a moment folding his arms and resting them on his belly. "First of all, of course it can be, it is possible, just not probable. And secondly, it's none of your business."

"Excuse me?"

"I believe I was very clear JJ."

"After all that I have told you about my own life, about all that I have been through, you won't even tell me why you *probably* took the name Banquo when you died?"

"OK. Well put. First, tell me why you want to know."

"Why? Well..." I had to think for a moment. I really wanted to know, but hadn't thought it through. I should have known better than to ask Banquo a question that wasn't well thought out, that I wasn't prepared to defend. After a moment he turned as if to leave and I said, "Look. You have been kind enough to teach me, to give me advice, to mentor me. Knowing something about you, what motivates you to do what you do, seems like a perfectly reasonable request."

"Very well," he said. And then there was silence; his face fell and looked as if he was remembering something that wasn't all that pleasant. "I didn't take the name Banquo; it was a nick-name I was given by some of the professors I worked with. Some of my students used it too, referring to me as Professor Banquo. After I died—"

"In the plane crash, right?" I interjected trying to draw out more of what I thought was sure would be very little information.

"—yes, after I died in the plane crash and found myself a ghost, I just kept using that name. It just made sense."

"And…"

"And what?"

"And what is your real name? When did you die? Why are you always so damn mysterious?"

Banquo chuckled, and leveled his appraising gaze at me. I felt as if he was weighing me or measuring me, seeing if I was worthy of more information. He turned and as he walked away he said, "One step at a time JJ. One step at a time."

I spent about two more weeks in the graveyard recuperating. Almost every day I would stumble across Motor, and always come away from our encounters in better shape, and at night I would go to the Midnight Circle and revel in the tragedies (and other works) of William Shakespeare as performed by ghosts. At the end of that time I was back to having a crisp solid form and was starting to gain my other skills back. That is when I went to visit Nate.

Transmission #60
Received 2010/12/19 03:15:41

Nate was home and, like me, mostly recovered from his wounds. My abilities were coming back, but my stamina was still really poor. I had to fade often. I had finally come to peace with fading—I didn't fight it anymore. It was short term oblivion, and that had come to suit me just fine.

I flew in just before midnight when I was strongest and found him sitting in a chair in front of his trailer, out under the stars. His hair was very short, his face looked drawn and he had lost weight. He looked terrible, but his appearance was neat and clean and no beer bottles were in sight.

I modulated my hand to produce a light (albeit a weak one) and flew it in a circle in front of him.

"Thank God!" he exclaimed. "Can we talk?"

I flashed the light up and down: *YES.*

I followed him inside where he booted the laptop and turned off all the lights.

"Are you OK?" he asked.

RECOVERING. YOU?

"Recovering, yeah that's a good word for it. Not back to

work yet, but starting to feel like myself again." Nate paused, his face graying, "I... I...." he stammered.

NOT TIME 4 U 2 GO.

"Yeah. Yeah, that's it. I'm done with that. Look JJ, I just had a moment there... I lost it... and you..." He paused, his eyes growing damp. "I can't believe what you did man. You saved my life."

WHAT R FRIENDS 4?

"Seriously JJ. You scared the shit out of me lighting up like the Human Torch or something. How the hell did you do that?"

ELECTRICITY LOTS OF IT.

"I was so worried, I don't know what it is like over there— could you have... err... died?"

COULD HAVE MOVED ON.

"Shit! Look, I am getting help, seeing a therapist. I am still a mess but I'm gonna get through this. You've got to promise no more of that kind of stuff."

PROMISE.

Nate sighed.

I paused; I had come here to say something and was finding it hard to say. Keeping the light up was draining me quick and I didn't have long so I got to it.

U GOTTA GRIEVE. I GOTTA GRIEVE. NO OTHER WAY.

Nate nodded his head in assent, but said nothing.

I HAVE 2 GO. CANT STICK AROUND. NOT GOOD 4 U. NOT GOOD 4 ME.

Nate nodded his head again as tears ran down his face, "I know bro, I know."

I left then; I couldn't stand to sit there watching him cry. I couldn't stand what I was feeling either, but I could no longer deny it. My life as I knew it was over. I couldn't spend any more time denying it, or being angry about it, or being depressed. It was time to accept it, and feel it—all of it.

I wanted to do one more thing before fully moving on from my old life. I needed to finish my story so I flew off to the university and spent some time in the chamber.

Interview Transcript
Janet Lynch / Nate Luca: Part 14

Tamara: We're almost to the end. Can you both comment on the document as a whole?

Janet: Can I have a copy? There is so much I don't understand—I need to read it myself.

Tamara: Not yet, I am sorry. When we get ready to publish it, you two will be the first to get copies.

Janet: Oh.

Tamara: Can you comment? Do you believe that your son wrote this and that these incidents occurred?

Janet: What? Yes. Of course, yes. My boy is a ghost (shaking head).

Tamara: Nate?

Nate: Yes, this is JJ. Everything he described regarding me occurred.

Tamara: Thank you.

Transmission #61
Received 2010/12/20 00:12:32

So we have finally come to the end of the story. Frankly I am surprised there is so much of it, who knew it would take so many words to talk about something so ordinary (death, that is)? I am hopeful that this will one day see the light of day, and my story will help others.

Jesus, Banquo, and I are teaming up and going off on an adventure. We each need to move on: Jesus needs to wrap up his life; Banquo is in need of a new challenge—I think in some way my daredevil stunts have opened his eyes to what it is possible to do from this side; and I need to completely separate from my old life, besides I feel I owe Jesus for all his help.

Jesus doesn't feel right with his murderer running around loose. Since he is the only one that knows what his killer looks like, and neither of us knows how to pop yet, we're going to track him down the old-fashioned way. Jesus has spent the last month picking up his very cold trail and is anxious to get started. I have been working hard on finishing this story so I can leave with a clear conscience.

I expect I'll be away for a while, maybe for good. Tam and Jin, do me a favor, and get this to Ma and Nate. I know you have protocols for publication, need for rigor, and stuff like that, but they need this. They will keep it quiet. They will also be able to verify some of the things that are written here, that this is me. Further proof of life beyond death—woooooooooooo! Maybe you can make them a part of the project.

It has been a strange path to acceptance around my death, and my life, but I am glad I am finally getting there. I am no longer naive enough to think the path is a straight one or has a definite end. This is not some storybook "...and they lived happily ever after," it is not that plain or simple. Acceptance isn't the end, it isn't perfection, it's just "acceptance." Yeah, I lost my dad and was looped for a while; yeah, I lost Rhiannon; yeah, I died at the hands of some drunk fools and nearly killed one of them; yeah, I nearly drove my best friend to suicide; and yeah, I killed a man. But through it all, I did my best and I am OK. I am still here.

Don't freak, OK? I am not saying acceptance is a free pass out of past mistakes. I still regret many of the things I did and I am still striving to do better. But what is different is that I can now accept the reality of my life and death and still function, still move on.

I think what it comes down to is this: the grief and trauma doesn't go away, it just stops defining you, stops controlling you.

So life goes on, even after you are dead, and I am off to live it. I've got friends, and I've got acceptance, and I've got purpose, what more could I need?

It was a hell of a life, and it is turning into a hell of an afterlife.

This is Joseph Jeffery Lynch signing off.

Epilogue One

As Tamara stopped reading, a silence descended upon the little room. Nate sat uncomfortably, his hands alternated between rubbing his legs and being folded under his arms. Janet sat stock still, tears running down her face. Tamara shifted in her seat, moving as if to put the papers down on the floor and then clutching them to her chest. Jin moved nervously among the equipment.

"Well," Janet said, finally breaking the silence.

"I'll say," Nate added, with a small laugh.

"Indeed," Janet said, a small laugh escaping her.

"Without a doubt," Nate continued, his laugh growing.

"No shit," Tamara said, as she too started to laugh.

"No shit!" Janet echoed, her laugh growing large and full.

The laughter caught and swept everyone up. It bounced from person to person. When it seemed like it would die down, another of the four would start laughing again and the other three would join in. They all laughed, tears running down their faces, until their bellies hurt and they could laugh no more.

Janet took a deep breath, wiping the tears from her face.

"Can you shut the video off?"

"Sure," Tamara said, signaling to Jin who went to each camera shutting them down.

"What are you going to do with this?" Janet asked.

"We are going to finish our interviews and publish it," Tamara said. "Try to get funding to continue our work, see if we can get transmissions from other ECs."

"Is anyone going to believe it?" Janet asked.

Tamara shrugged, "Some will."

"Enough will," Nate added.

"This calls for a toast," Janet declared. She got up and went to the kitchen pulling a bottle of champagne out of the refrigerator and four glasses from a cabinet. She handed the bottle to Nate, "If you will do the honors."

Nate popped the cork and poured champagne into the glasses lifting his and saying, "To JJ." The rest echoed saying, "To JJ."

"Gone, but not forgotten," Jin said, raising his glass.

"Not really gone at all," Janet added. The glasses clinked and they drank.

Anna-Beth Smithson was nervous. She gripped the folder in her lap tightly, her palms sweaty in spite of the air-conditioner blowing on her. "She knows what happened," she said to William Arthur Reynolds who drove the car.

William shrugged his shoulders and did not comment.

"She read that document that he wrote, the *whole* document," Anna-Beth said licking her lips, "she knows every-thing."

"Damn it, Anna, we have talked about this over and over. It was a steering malfunction, a horrible accident. A tragedy, yes, but there is nothing to know."

Anna-Beth sat there silent, sullen.

"This is your idea," William said. "This making amends thing."

"It doesn't matter if it was a steering malfunction or not, the fact is a man died, we can't just let that pass." The image of his body passed before her eyes. She breathed deeply, as she had been taught, letting the thought fade without pushing it away.

"I know, I know," William said. "We have been over this. What has happened to you?"

"What do you mean?"

"You used to be so much *fun*."

"You're an ass, William, you know that? What the hell do you think happened to me? A man died, haunted us, almost killed me, and talked to me while I was having a near death experience."

William shook his head. "Six months ago you had never even given one thought to death or what happens after we die."

She paused, thinking. He was right. She had changed, and unfortunately he hadn't. She loved him but... She didn't allow herself to finish the thought. "Look Will, I need to do this, that is all you need to know."

They drove in silence the rest of the way to the apartment complex, got out and made their way to the door. Anna-Beth pushed the door bell, her heart pounding in her ears.

Janet Lynch opened the door and said, "Anna-Beth? William?"

"Yes," Anna-Beth said.

"Please, come in."

She followed Janet into the living room where a big man with his arms folded stood. "This is Nate, JJ's best friend.

Nate, this is Anna-Beth and William." They all shook hands when she added, "Would you like some tea?"

"Yes, thank you," Anna-Beth said. Janet left the room and she sat next to William on the couch across from the chair Nate sat in. She was nervous, her mouth dry. "So, the weather's pretty nice, not too hot."

"Yup," Nate said.

Help me out William, she thought, but he just sat there not making eye contact. "They say that summer is going to come early this year—they are already talking about wildfires."

"Umm. Hmmm."

Damn it Will! She took a deep breath, remembering why she was there, why this was important. "So you knew JJ a long time?"

"Met him in the 6th grade."

"You were close?"

Nate paused looking at her, hard. His eyes lingered on her face, her nose. She felt self-conscious as if under a microscope. "What?" she asked, touching her hair.

"Your nose," Nate said, "he was right about your nose."

"My nose?"

"In that document he wrote—you read it right?" She nodded her head. "He said your nose had a crink in it, he was right."

She blushed, looking to William, but his head was down, his fingers playing with his shoe laces. Her hand rose to her nose, "I... I... guess."

"It suits you," he said. Her blushed deepened.

She was saved from saying anything else by the arrival of the tea. After tea had been served, Janet sat in a chair next to Nate and said, "So, what can I do for you, Anna-Beth?"

"Umm…" she began, "I… We… We just want to express our deepest condolences for your loss."

A shadow flickered across Janet's face that was quickly replaced by a small upturning of her thin lips. "Thank you."

Anna-Beth looked to William, but he was still looking down. "William…" she said.

"I am sorry for your loss," he said his head coming up and his eyes making brief contact with Janet's.

"That is kind of you William. Thank you."

"We would like to do something to memorialize your son." She was met by silence so she forged on. "We know nothing can bring him back…"

Nate's eyes teared up as Janet openly wept, they both remained silent.

I knew this wasn't going to be easy, she thought, *deep breath.* "I know that remembering the best about him is important. That is why I wanted to talk to you." She pulled some papers out of the folder she had been clutching in her lap, got up, and handed them to Janet and Nate. "We want to do something that honors his memory. We have started raising some funds and there are a few ideas in there: a scholarship fund; land conservation; and a few others."

She paused, giving them time to read, and herself time to breath. "We want to do something that would make sense to him. What did JJ love?"

"Cars," Nate said.

"Cars?" Anna-Beth asked.

"Yeah," Nate said, "mainly fixing them and taking them apart. His hands, he loved to work with his hands." Janet nodded in agreement.

"OK, we can work with that. How about something to teach kids how to fix cars?"

The discussion took off from there and Anna-Beth was relieved, she had been able to take action, to do something. It felt good. William even got involved in the discussion; maybe there was hope for him yet.

An hour later as they walked back to their car she said, "See?"

"What?" William asked.

"That wasn't so bad."

"Speak for yourself."

"You can't tell me you don't feel just a little bit good."

"Maybe, but just a little." He held up his thumb and finger very close together.

She punched him in the shoulder, laughing.

Epilogue Two

Janet Lynch was dying. She had felt it coming on for a long time. She wasn't scared, she wasn't sad, she was curious. Having outlived her husband by twenty-seven years and her son JJ by twenty-two, she thought her seventy-four years was a good run, a good amount of time to have lived.

The pain had been the toughest part. Cancer eating away at her organs was no fun, but finally she was getting some relief. She laid in a bed, in a small room of the hospice, morphine coursing through her veins. Lacy curtains let sun flow into the room.

They had a beautiful garden here, but it had been days since she had the energy go out there. She was spending more time sleeping, more time dreaming.

"Hi, Ma," Nate said from the door. He was still a big man, but his hair was graying, his forehead was wrinkled, and crow's feet decorated his eyes.

"Nate," Janet said. "So good of you to come."

"Of course." He walked over and kissed her cheek.

"Where is my daughter-in-law? Where are my grandchildren?"

"Sorry, they couldn't make it today; it's just the two of us."

"Oh, nice. That's good. I get you all to myself." She reached out and took his hand, feeling the warmth, holding it as tightly as she could.

She dozed off. Nate was still there when she woke, looking at her.

"What?" she asked.

"Just thinking," Nate said.

"About JJ?"

"Yeah."

"Think he'll be there when I go?" Janet asked.

"If he can, you know he will."

"I wouldn't mind seeing Hamlet performed by ghosts."

Nate chuckled, "Me neither."

They were silent for a time. "I am not worried about the dreams."

"Dreams?" Nate asked.

"*For in the sleep of death what dreams may come, when we have shuffled off this mortal coil.* You know, from Hamlet, those dreams."

"No, that wouldn't make any sense."

"No it wouldn't. JJ showed the way."

Author's Note

Thank you so much for reading. What follows is an excerpt from *To Be a Fool*, the sequel to this book, and then acknowledgements and a bit about me.

But, before you proceed, I have a favor to ask you. If you've enjoyed this book, then do me the honor of spreading the word. Write an honest review on Amazon (just a few sentences is fine), loan the book, or tell your friends. Word of mouth is the best endorsement a book can get, and only you can do that. Thank you!

For more ghostly adventures (and cameos from JJ, Jesus, and Banquo), check out *Drawing the Dead*. Or pick up *Life After*, a collection of short stories that features a brand new ghost trying to solve his own murder.

Curious about Jesus and his past? Well, the third Ghost Memoir book, *Of Things Not Seen*, will be told by Jesus.

If you want to know as soon as new books come out please sign up for my email newsletter. Go to RobertJMcCarter.com, you'll see the signup offer on the home page. As of this writing I am giving away ebooks of the first episode of my Superhero/Love Story series.

Want more of the adventures of JJ, Jesus, Banquo and the gang? The following is a sample of To Be a Fool.

Prologue

NATE LUCA PACED AS JIN SHI AND TAMARA WATSON set up the video gear. He was nervous. As a friend, Nate knew that at times you signed yourself up for some hard duty. As a best friend, even more so. And even though Nate's best friend, JJ Lynch, was dead, was a ghost, Nate was still obliged to him. Obliged to do what was right, to do what he needed to do.

He paused, rubbing his sweating palms on his jeans and tucking his white T-shirt in again for the fourth time. "Is there a problem?" he asked.

Jin mumbled something that Nate couldn't hear, and Tamara stepped away and walked over to Nate. "It's just not turning on. The battery is fine, but it won't come on." Nate studied her expression as she spoke. It lacked any trace of surprise.

Nate looked around the mostly empty building that housed Afterlife Communications. It had tall ceilings and a concrete floor. The kind of place you might find used as an auto shop or a small printer. In one corner sat the SECI chamber, the device JJ had used to communicate with them and to write his memoir. Next to it were the skeletons of two more SECI chambers in the process of being built. SECI: The Search for Extra-Corporeal Intelligence. It is a project that Tamara and Jin had started at the University of Arizona (UA) and now were taking private. The three SECI chambers and the adjoining offices were the start of Afterlife Communications, Inc.

"Do you think it's a ghost?" Nate asked, a shiver going down his spine. He knew enough to justify his concern.

Tamara shrugged and smiled, as if having a ghost interfere with her electronics was the most normal thing in the world. "Could be. Just be patient, Nate, we'll get it going. We've got another camera we can dig out if this one doesn't respond soon."

"It's just—" Nate began.

"I know, Nate, I know," she said, her hand lightly touching his muscular arm. "It's a hell of thing to have to tell him."

Nate nodded, "Rhiannon... I just can't believe it. She's so young. I'm afraid of how he'll react. He'll probably lose it." Nate paused as he stared at the SECI chamber. "Do you think he'll be back? Do you think he'll get the message in time?"

Tamara ran her hands through her shoulder-length black hair, pulling it back into a ponytail. "I hope so. We've got the 2.0 SECI chamber up and running for him. I hope he finds it and uses it. And if he does, this video will be in the chamber with instructions for him on how to trigger it and he'll hear what you need to tell him."

Nate nodded again, retucking his shirt in for the fifth time. It fit tightly across his broad chest. "Thanks for letting me do the greeting."

"Of course, Nate. You have some important news, it's

only right. Do you remember what to say?"

Nate pulled the piece of paper out of his back pocket, his eyes scanning the notes. "Yeah, I've got it. I'll tell him this stuff first, before—"

"Got it!" Jin shouted from behind the camera. "Let's do this before it decides to turn itself off again."

Video Transcript #1

Nate Luca speaking to JJ Lynch
Recorded on 2011/10/16 2:13 p.m.
Playback triggered on 2012/01/11 9:15 p.m.

HEY, BRO, WELCOME BACK. JIN AND TAMARA ARE LETTING me do this introduction for you. They first asked me to write it, but you know me. Unlike you, I couldn't write my way out of a paper bag—it would take me days to write this down. And it would be even harder to tell you...

But, I'm getting ahead of myself. I'm here to introduce you to SECI 2.0 and to give you some news.

Since your book, *Shuffled Off*, came out SECI has taken off. There are lots of ghosts trying their hand at the SECI Chamber and a few are even able to use it. They are getting transmissions in all the time. Tamara got worried that with the traffic in the chamber now you would have trouble getting through if you wanted to. And everyone wants to hear from you again.

So we were having dinner one night and Tam and Jin were talking about making another chamber for you and hiding it so the other ghosts couldn't find it. They were talking about a few improvements, and I suggested they make you a real keyboard. Like when you made that little light and hovered it over the keys to my laptop, back when you first started to communicate with me. I thought it would be easier than making all those crazy symbols you had to make for the original SECI chamber.

Well, they liked the idea, and here we are. SECI 2.0. It's just like a big keyboard and any unusual electromagnetic radiation in the rectangle of the key will register the corresponding letter. It should be a lot easier on you and a lot quicker.

So, that's the intro, and now I have some news for you.

I won't lie to you. It's been tough. I've been in counseling since... since... God, JJ, that night. I don't really even know how to talk about it. I was crazy with grief and then you showed up and started to communicate with me. Well, I was off my nut thinking that I wanted to be a ghost too. That druggy tried to steal the tow truck and what did I do? I tried to get him to shoot me. And he would have killed me, but you tapped into the electricity of the Prius and moved his hand just enough so he didn't shoot me in the head. He died from electrocution, you nearly destroyed your ghostly form, and I nearly died from the gunshot wound to my chest.

It's been over a year and I still have nightmares about that night. About what I almost did and what you did do to save me. I...

I miss you, man. I miss you bad. I mean, it is comforting knowing you are out there, but I miss sitting and talking with you. Working on cars. Having a beer or two. Hanging out.

But, you know, things are getting better. Slowly, but

surely, they are getting better.

Your mother, Ma, is doing good. Not "good" in the sense of skipping around and singing, but good in the sense of having buried both her husband and her son and getting her feet under her. She's got a part-time job and does some volunteer work. I'd tell you more, but I know she would rather do it herself. Once we know you're back, Tam and Jin will get her in here to record a video for you.

Speaking of volunteering. I am on the board of the "JJ Lynch Foundation." Anna-Beth and William—well, mostly Anna-Beth—have started a foundation in your name. Who would have thought this would come out of them being in the car that killed you.

They've collected a lot of money, and we are going to help "at-risk" teens with vocational education. Sounds fancy, but basically we are going to teach troubled kids to fix cars. Get them dirty, give them something to do.

This is all Anna-Beth, bro. What she went through with you, what happened with you and her... Well, it changed her in a big way. She's... She's...

God I wish you were here. I wish we could talk about shit like this. I am doing my best to implement the patented "JJ Lynch's slowly grow on them" method, but there are some subtleties I am not sure of. I enjoy spending time with her and I am doing my best to be her friend and let things go from there. But...

William is still in the picture, but I don't think for much longer. Maybe they'll break up, and I'll be there like you were for Rhiannon...

Shit, JJ, this is so damn hard. Tam isn't letting me do this so I can babble on about Ma and me, about the little pieces of our lives. She is letting me do this because I have something important to say. Something I would love not to have to tell you.

It's Rhiannon, bro, she's real sick. I... You...

Ah, hell. This sucks. She's got a tumor in her brain. It's got some damn fancy name that I can't remember, but it's killing her, bro. It's killing her.

They discovered it about eight months ago. She had surgery and chemo and it looked pretty good, but it's back now, and they're saying they can't operate. They're gonna do radiation, but reading between the lines, it's not hopeful. This thing is a killer, almost no one survives it for very long.

I'm so sorry to be the bearer of these bad tidings. I can just imagine how you are feeling. But listen to me, I know it hurts but you've got to take care of yourself. Don't go all JJ-apeshit on me. Don't go doing crazy things.

Look, the reason I am telling you this is... Well, because I know you would want to know. But, also, so maybe you can be there if she does... you know... die. You can be there to help her along if she's earth-bound like you. If she's a ghost.

I can't imagine you wouldn't want to be there. So, in case you haven't mastered traveling, that "popping" thing you talked about in your book, Jin is going to put some maps on the end of this. She's still in Texas, and the maps will show you how to get to her.

I am going to keep tabs on things and go out there at some point before...

Take care of yourself, bro, and keep your head on.

I sure hope you come back. I hope you get this message in time. I hope you're OK.

Transmission #1

Received 2012/01/11 21:42:03

THIS IS JOSEPH JEFFERY LYNCH. I DON'T KNOW WHAT TO say. I have so much to say. So much has happened, but I just saw the video of Nate talking about Rhiannon.

The world doesn't ever stop, does it? Not for a damn minute. Not for anything, and certainly not when you need it the most.

Tam, I've got your fiancé John here. I found him, I... well, it's why I came back. He's the reason you started the SECI project, the reason I can write my stories, but... It's a long story and I'd love to tell it to you... I'd love to...

Listen, I have to go. I can't stay here banging on your ghost keyboard when Rhiannon might be dying or be...

Now if that isn't something, here I am a ghost and I don't want to say the word 'dead.' Unbelievable.

OK, this is hitting me now. I'm a mess but I don't want to leave you hanging too badly, Tam, so here's a message from John.

"Honey, I'm OK. I am so very, very sorry for what happened and how it happened. That you saw me die that way, that I left so many things unsaid. JJ will come back with me later and we'll tell you the whole story. For now just know that I love you and I'm OK."

I'm starting to lose it here. I'm going to get John back to the graveyard and go find Rhiannon. Alive or dead, I'm going to find her. I'll be back as soon as I can.

Transmission #2

Received 2012/01/30 01:12:42

I'M BACK AND I HAVE A STORY TO TELL, BUT BEFORE I start I need to get something off my chest. Something that I must say and I hope that you will indulge me.

Life is grief.

Think about it, it is. Not in a "hide my head in the sand and be depressed for the rest of my existence" way. No, not like that. But like gravity. As in the natural order of things, as in, just the way it is and there is nothing you can do about it.

Like gravity, you can fight it, you can expend tremendous energy and counteract its forces briefly, but no matter how hard you try it's not going to go away, it's not going to change, and there is not a damn thing you can do about it.

Grief is a natural reaction to change. Things change and we grieve. That crappy old dorm room you left for your first professional job. You think you're done, you're glad to be out, but you sometimes miss it. You miss the simplicity of life in college that the dorm room represented. You miss the goofy stoner who lived across the hall from you and told the worst jokes. You miss the boneheads pulling the fire alarm in the middle of the night because you had some of the best conversations of your life while half-awake in the quad under the moonlight.

You grieve the end of that life even as you are excited about the beginning of a new one. Change results in grief. There is no getting out of it—just like gravity.

And in life there is no getting out of change, no matter how hard you try. And believe me, I was the expert at resisting change, floating along in my life like a rudderless ship just hoping nothing bad happened. Doesn't matter, change comes. Change came to me when my dad died, change came when Rhiannon, the love of my life, kicked me out, and change certainly came when a car full of drunk coeds slammed into me, killing me instantly.

Life = Change. Change = Grief. Life = Grief.

You can pretend otherwise, but you know what that is gonna cause you? More grief.

I apologize if this kind of rambling isn't what you were looking for. I really do. I know you want to hear cool stories about ghostly powers, graveyards, and grand adventures. And those are coming, and I fully understand if you need to skip ahead a few pages. But indulge me. I feel the need to set the stage like the narrator does at the beginning of Romeo and Juliet. I am your humble thespian laying out the view of the landscape we are about to cover.

So before we get to the grand adventure and breathless realizations, I need to step onto my soapbox for a moment. What? You think that bit I just said was me on my soapbox. Nope, but here it is.

It's hard when someone you care for dies. So hard. It is

a broad spectrum of reactions that goes from an emotional hiccup, to the shape of your life never being the same again.

If it's a big change, grief is required. One way or another, whether healthy or not, you will grieve. No choice. It's like gravity, remember?

So here comes the soapbox part. When it comes to grief, you, the living, have it easy.

I don't care if it was your firstborn child, a career, a cherished dream, or your partner of fifty years. You have it easy.

Now wait, before you throw the book across the room, let me explain. It's not that grieving the death of your child or your lifelong partner is easy. It is anything but. It is just not nearly as hard as dying.

Here's the thing. In most cases you lose one thing at a time. Your life may be changed, your world may be rocked, but it's usually one thing at a time. Not always, and I am not speaking in absolutes here, I am just pointing out that the scale goes higher, much higher, than what the living regularly experience.

When someone dies they aren't giving up one person, they are giving up *every* person. When someone dies they aren't giving up a job or hobby or dream, but *every* job and *every* hobby and *every* dream. When someone dies they aren't losing one thing, they are losing *every*-thing.

Sure, plenty of souls move directly on and don't end up as an earth-bound spirit, or a ghost, like me, but the ones that do end up as ghosts are on that far end of the spectrum of grief. Is it any wonder that so many of us end up as slack-jawed apparitions stuck in our own personal hell? We call that place the "bardo" around the graveyard.

Think about it. Did you like to read? Well, you can't turn pages anymore, making reading quite difficult. Were you a writer? Well, except for the SECI project that is enabling me to type this manuscript, you are out of luck. Did you garden, play sports, love to go shopping? Nope, can't do that here. Did you love facebook or twitter, or fooling around at your computer? That's gone too. Did you value the kindness and support of friends, having long conversations with them over food and drinks, roughhousing with your kids? Gone, gone, gone.

Look, I am in no way trying to minimize the grief you have been through. I had some whoppers in my day when I was still corporeal. I am just trying to give you a sense of scale, of perspective.

And one other thing. Someday a friend of yours or a family member is going to have a slow death. That person is going to have some time to think about all this, to get their affairs in order, and to say their good-byes (or not). And that friend or family member will be going through a lot—really as much as you can go through.

And you will be going through your own experiences around their upcoming transition. You will be having a difficult time, you will be seeing ahead to a life that is barely recognizable. You, in a word, will be grieving.

When this happens—and if you are lucky enough to stay in a body long enough, it *will* happen—remember how much more that dying person is giving up. While you are about to give them up, they are about to give up *everything*.

One moment they will be alive, and the next moment they will be dead and gone. And when that happens your life will be changed, but their life, as we commonly define it, will be over.

So if they grow withdrawn and distant, and you need to be close; if they need to talk, and you need to be quiet;

if they want to pretend it's not happening, and you don't; if they need to share feelings, and you need to bottle it all in—go with it. If whatever they do gets in the way of your grieving, do one thing for me. Get Over It. I am not saying to not have your process, to not grieve, to not try to get your needs met. I am saying put the dying person first. What the dying says goes. End of story. Period.

Yes, your world is about to change, maybe beyond recognition. But their world, it's about to end.

It's not like when you left college and started work, or when you had your first child, or when your kids left the house for good. Sure, your world changes in a huge way, but many things stay the same. Like your family and friends, your history and abilities, your hopes and dreams. It's not like that when you die. Everything changes, even down to the laws that govern the world you are living in.

It's a lot. That's all I'm saying. It's a hell of a lot.

Transmission #3

Received 2012/01/30 03:11:16

OK, NOW THAT I'VE GOT THAT OFF MY CHEST, I GUESS I should back up, back way up.

My name is Joseph Jeffery Lynch, but everyone calls me JJ. I died on August 22, 2010, when a car full of drunk coeds plowed into me, pinning me to the jungle gym at a Mickey D's.

I found myself a ghost and went through a lot coming to accept that and dealing with the life that I had left behind and my loved ones. I've already written about all of that so I won't go into it now.

I'm back because... well... I'm back because so much has happened, and the last time I did this it really helped me to get my head screwed back on.

To belabor the metaphor, my head is anything but screwed on right now. I am a huge mess. I have promised to tell the story of John for Tamara, so I was going to come here and do just that and nothing else. Let John talk, say what he needs to say, and just type it out.

But Banquo wouldn't hear of it. Banquo is… well, I guess you would call him my mentor. He is the one that has been showing me and my best dead friend Jesus the ropes.

Jesus's name is pronounced "Hey-Zues," not "Gee-Zus," as he is often fond of saying when he explains the pronunciation, "I don't want be confused with the big fellow."

You see, ghosts like me can move on. Moving "on" is a euphemism around here for, well, moving on to the next level. And just like the living talking about dying, there isn't too much of a consensus about what that "moving on" is, just that it's the next step. Those who die at peace move on right away and don't end up like us ghosts. But moving on, answering the Call, is generally accepted to be a good thing, the next step. But I am not ready to answer the Call, I don't want to move on, I don't want to leave this world yet. And while I am here, I want to do something worth doing.

So I asked Banquo to be my mentor, to train me, to take me on as his apprentice. If I'm here, if I'm a ghost, I want to do things that matter. But, you see, I'm still kind of a mess from what I've just been through. Me being here and writing this is my way of processing it all, of getting over it, of grieving. And Banquo won't teach me until I'm done.

Banquo used to be a professor of English Literature, and he has structured lessons he teaches to the newly dead, like me. His lessons are: 1) Cutting the Cord; 2) Appearance Matters; 3) Awareness, Awareness, Awareness; 4) Traveling; and 5) This is Not the End.

I am badly stuck on Lesson #4 and am eager to figure that one out. It is really a pain to have to fly everywhere and not be able to "pop" from place to place like most everyone else.

So, I'm going to be here day in and day out until I tell

my story, until I can get some perspective, until I can move past it.

To be honest, I don't know if what I am doing is a good idea. I mean, it's good for me, but I worry about what it means for the world, for those that believe, for those that come to know there is an afterlife. It's heady stuff, and frankly more philosophical than I am suited for, but the question rumbles around my mind. What happens when people "know" there is an afterlife and just don't "believe" it? There is a huge difference between believing and knowing, and I am not so big a fool that I don't know that such a transition could get messy.

So here I am and there is so much to tell. As I flew over I thought about how to tell the story and make it understandable. I really want to leap ahead and talk about Rhiannon, but honestly I think that it is too fresh and that I will lose my way if I try to do that. So, I am going to start right where the last story ended. I'll take you through the whole thing and hopefully it will all make sense.

That's the end of the sample. To find out what happens next, pick up a copy of To Be a Fool. *For more information go to:*

RobertJMcCarter.com/Books/ToBeAFool

Acknowledgements

Great love and gratitude to my wife, Aleia, without whom I would not be who I am today.

Special thanks to Wayne who shuffled off far too soon for all of us left behind. Your courageous journey continues to teach and inspire. Without what we experienced this book would not exist. Love you man.

Love and thanks to Jeff; you always trusted me, even when we hardly knew each other. I think you would like this book, and without your departure, and what I went through after it, this book would not be. In many ways this is your book; not about you, but because of you.

Many, many thanks to my fabulous team of beta readers: John Bifano, Peter Klein, Michele Lytle, Gary D. McClellan, Aleia N. O'Reilly, Eliot Schipper, and Janine Schipper. Your enthusiasm and feedback blew me away. You made this a better book.

Thanks to Diana Cox who proofread for me. She does it professionally and you can email her at support@novelproofreading.com, or visit her web page at www.novelproofreading.com. Her work was great and her rates reasonable; I highly recommend her.

I want to thank and acknowledge the characters in this book (JJ, Jesus, Banquo, Nate, Janet, Anna-Beth, William, Tamara, Jin and all the rest). Thank you for letting me tell your story. I know that may sound weird, but honestly I often didn't feel like I was writing this book. My task was to listen carefully and to follow the characters (and they often, to my great delight, led me to places I didn't expect). These characters feel real to me, and I hope they feel real to you.

Finally, thank you dear reader. My hope is that you found the journey rewarding.

About the Author

ROBERT J. MCCARTER IS THE AUTHOR OF FIVE NOVELS, three novellas, and dozens of short stories. He is a finalist for the *Writers of the Future* context and his stories have appeared in *Adomeda Spaceways Inflight Magazine*, *Everyday Fiction*, and numerous anthologies. His short stories have been published alongside such luminaries as Brandon Sanderson, Peter S. Beagle, Jody Lynn Nye, and David Farland.

He has written a series of first person ghost novels (starting with *Shuffled Off: A Ghost's Memoir*) and a superhero / love story series (*Neutrinoman and Lightningirl: A Love Story*). Ten of his short stories were published in *Life After: Stories of Life, Death, and the Places In Between*.

He lives in the mountains of Arizona with his amazing wife and his ridiculously adorable dog. Find out more at RobertJMcCarter.com.

Books by Robert J. McCarter

Novels in the "Ghost's Memoir" world:
Shuffled Off: A Ghost's Memoir, Book 1
Drawing the Dead
To Be a Fool: A Ghost's Memoir, Book 2
Of Things Not Seen: A Ghost's Memoir, Book 3

Books in the Neutrinoman and Lightningirl Series:
Meteor Attack!
Lightningirl and Neutrinoman, A Love Story. Episode 1
Toxic Asset
Lightningirl and Neutrinoman, A Love Story. Episode 2
Protocol X
Lightningirl and Neutrinoman, A Love Story. Episode 3
Season 1 (Omnibus edition of Episodes 1 - 3)
Off Book
Lightningirl and Neutrinoman, A Love Story. Episode 4
(Coming soon)

Short Stores and Collections
Life After: Stories of Life, Death, and the Places in Between
Probability: Resolve
The Turing Test Will Be Televised
Ghost Hacker, Zombie Maker

For a complete list, go to RobertJMcCarter.com

www.ingramcontent.com/pod-product-compliance
Lightning Source LLC
Chambersburg PA
CBHW031549240626
47153CB00002B/439